A Wolf Tells Lies
© 2025 Alden Louper

All rights reserved. No part of this book may be reproduced, stored in a retrieval system, or transmitted in any form or by any means—electronic, mechanical, photocopying, recording, or otherwise without the prior written permission of the publisher, except in the case of brief quotations embodied in critical articles and reviews.

Published by Liko Forest Publishing
Paperback ISBN: 978-1-0684336-0-3
eBook ISBN: 978-1-0684336-1-0

This is a work of fiction. Names, characters, places, and incidents are either the product of the author's imagination or used fictitiously. Any resemblance to actual persons, living or dead, events, or locales is purely coincidental.

A WOLF TELLS LIES

Whispers of the Greater Ones test a young wolf's faith

Alden Louper

First instalment of **The Wolves of the Vale Rift**

Contents

1. Chapter 1 — 1
2. Chapter 2 — 17
3. Chapter 3 — 39
4. Chapter 4 — 59

Bridge — 77

5. Chapter 5 — 79
6. Chapter 6 — 95
7. Chapter 7 — 117
8. Chapter 8 — 135
9. Chapter 9 — 151
10. Chapter 10 — 171
11. Chapter 11 — 191
12. Chapter 12 — 209
13. Chapter 13 — 225

Dedicated to my mother, my aunt, and all of my friends who supported this project

Prologue

THE WORLD

The story begins in 1981, along the border of Wyoming and Montana, about two hundred miles east of Yellowstone. The region's geology is fictional — a vast, dense forest stretching across the land, sparsely inhabited by humans.

THE ALTERED TIMELINE

In this reimagined United States, the government-backed extermination program, aimed at protecting livestock by eradicating apex predators, was abandoned in the early 20th century. Humanity instead focuses their efforts on the many wars between 1910 and 1980.

Unlike our reality, wolves are thriving in a golden era, roaming freely through Wyoming, Montana, North and South Dakota, and Yellowstone National Park during the 1980s. With fewer poachers and a growing force of wildlife conservationists, the region's ecosystem is diverse, healthy, and teeming with life.

Wolves now dominate these lands as never before in Earth's history. Many wolf groups believe their ancestors are responsible for granting this newfound freedom. Yet, some still feel the fight is far from over...

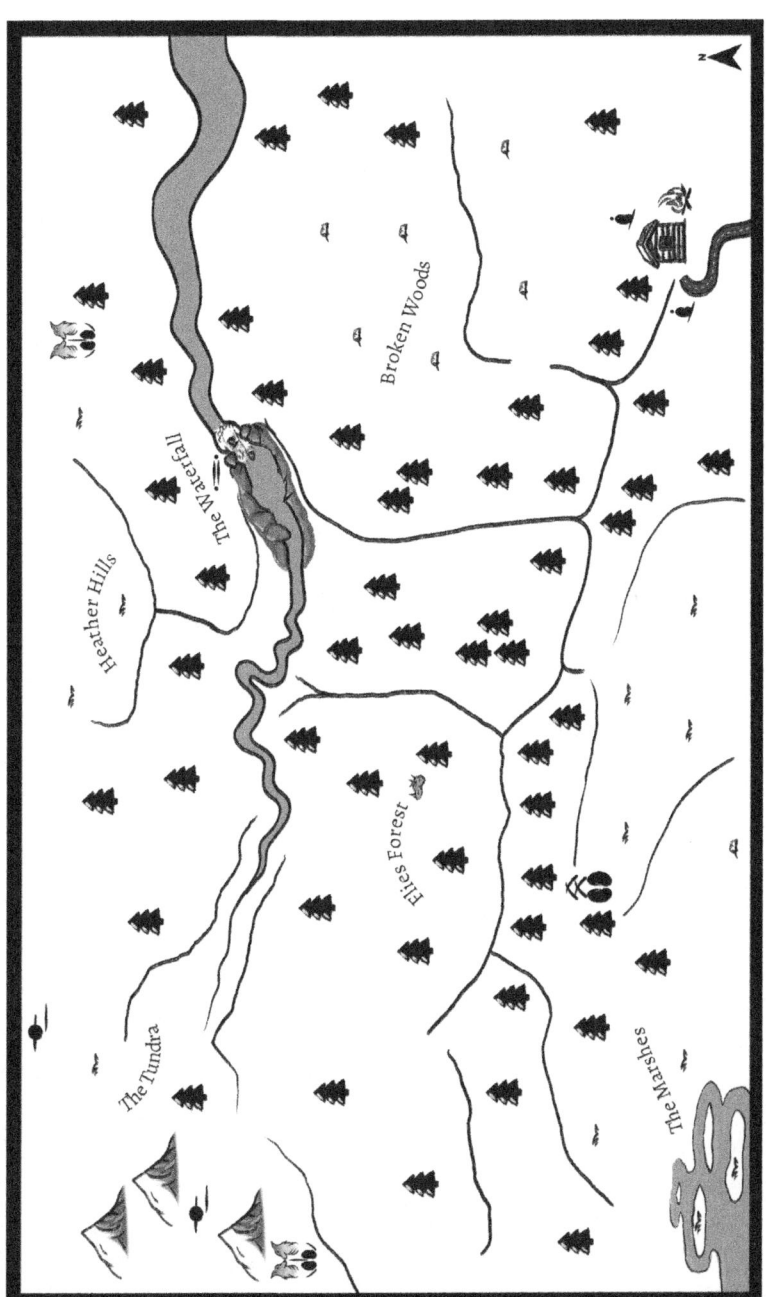

Chapter 1

A chilly wind drifted across the horizon. The many trees that covered the heather hills shook gently in the wake of the afternoon breeze. Winter was over and meadow bushes had sprouted their natural beauty into existence. The sun was in its' descent, following a cloudy and rainy morning. Its' light passed through the branches of the great oak trees. The wind feathered its way through the leaves and down to the light pockets of open space in the woods. It would stop upon hitting the thicket of bushes that housed goldenrod, lavender and beech leaves. The bristle they made in the wind was quickly suppressed by the chirping of afternoon birds, accompanied by the melody of bruxing bugs.

    An abrupt shake of green from a long leaf bush ceased the calmness, causing many birds to flock out of their homes in panic. Out of the leafy complex charged a tall wolf. His name was Wulfur. He was mostly a light brown with shades of timber glazed over his paws, snout, shoulders and tail. His ears were stripey and his back a dusty pattern of cocoa. Although he was rather lean around the belly, there was a lot of muscle on his chest and legs, with the rough waterproof pelt giving him an intimidating appearance when faced from the front.

He felt his shoulders stagger as he ascended the soiled slope. His footsteps were silent as he strode into the forest clearing. The big wolf's eyebrows lowered as he slowed his pace and glanced at the bush from where he came. Wulfur's tone of voice was slightly guttural and deep. He spoke with a slow and commanding rhythm to his trailing companion from behind the forage.

"This way, runt! Behind the rosemary bush. It'll mask our scent."

Without waiting for a response, the male wolf moved around the bush, his thick fur brushing against its leaves. There was also a large oak tree obstructing the hiding spot. He looked around, realising it was only spacious enough for him.

Wulfur peeked his head up and over the bush. *'Why is he so far behind?'* he thought. The wolf kept his attention on the gap he broke through moments ago. He could hear multiple howls, but they were very distant. *'That's the search party! For Likos' wits, hurry up, runt!'* The wolf tensed his shoulders and grunted aggressively to himself.

He waited, wondering if they were caught. He gave a narcissistic smirk at the open air, imagining what the wolves would do with the runt. Did they deserve it? Was he better off without them? He then let out a quiet sigh. Wulfur supposed that they didn't know any better. They were more than just a runt. More than just a random loner who tagged along with Wulfur to survive. This 'runt' was his son.

A moment of eerie silence broke through the clearing as Wulfur held his breath. Then his ears twitched forward. He picked up the faint sound of scampering claws against the dirty leaves. Wulfur then ducked his nose below the shrubbery, keeping an eye on the forage standing across from him.

Then a flash of golden fur blasted into the clearing. A much smaller skinnier male wolf with a short coat of dusty gold and white. His tail tip was black, and he had a deep brown stripe that bounced over his hip and connected at the rear, just like Wulfur's. His breath was anxious, head pivoting like a robin. His eyes were wide and had he a light tremble in his lips. He feathered his tongue between his teeth, looking around for something to speak to.

"Father?" he cried. "Where'd you go?"

"Here, now," Wulfur whispered back with a permanent grudge in his tone. He saw his son make eye contact with the lavender bush. Wulfur gave it a light shake. "Come around the bush, it's a bit tight, watch your-"

The timber wolf failed to finish his sentence. As he looked up, he saw his son leap toward him, dive over the bush and crash into its' stems. The runt had pressed against Wulfur's chest with his nose as he felt the leaves and stem tops cushion his landing. Bits of lavender were strewn around the shrub. Leaves were scattered and the golden wolf was leant over the bush like a puppy awaiting punishment.

Wulfur was fuming. Whilst the young male dangled headfirst toward the hiding spot, Wulfur got up on his hind paws and aggressively pressed his fronts into the runts' rump, forcing his body through the twigs. His son twitched and gritted his teeth as he felt twigs snap and puncture against his tummy, legs and groin.

"Aie! Oww! Wha-, mmphhh!" the runt winced and hissed under his breath.

"Shut up and stay down!" Wulfur ordered whilst holding his breath too. He concealed his son's tail into the bush and out of line of sight from the clearing. "Don't move. They'll hear us."

Wulfur then too pressed himself into a big fur loaf and leant against his son. The runt was squished between his hunched father and the stronger stalks of the shrubbery. He had nowhere to move without making a sound. So, he listened to his father and held his body completely still. His eyes were wincing hard, his breath heavy but suppressed through his nose.

Wulfur took a glance to the left and right of their hiding spot. This was it. He knew that if they were caught now, a wolf would surely die. And it was not going to be him.

Half a minute of silence passed. The runt moved his beady eyes up toward his father. Wulfur didn't look back at him and focused his senses on sound and smell. His ears moved smoothly, acting like radars. Watching this, his son ended up copying him.

Then a familiar rustle was heard. Another wolf! Wulfur didn't have a visual and tuned his ears to detect their movements. A skinny dark-grey wolf entered the clearing with his tail held high and eyes like stalks. He stopped in the middle, noticing the mess of twigs and flowers that now dotted the empty space between the tree trunks. He leant down and inhaled a whiff of the lavender. Wulfur could hear the intense sniffing from a few metres away.

From Wulfur's experiences, this type of flower had been used to mask up the scent of death. Wolves could hide a corpse with the purpose to have it never found. He figured it would be even more effective to block the scent of live wolves.

The grey chasing wolf lifted his head up and took a sniff of the air. His expression was mute and his eyes twitched, but he didn't step forward at all. He looked around for a moment taking in the sights of the area. Then he looked directly behind him from where he came to hear the muffled voices of his allies.

"Chief, this way! I think I'm onto something!"

The standing grey wolf sighed disapprovingly. He turned and padded back down the path he came from toward the sound of his search party. Wulfur's eyes then relaxed. His tense shoulders eased up as the sound of paw pads faded away.

Silence filled the forest void. That was when Wulfur unhunched himself from the bush and crawled gently into the opening. He breathed in through his nose, sensing relief. They were gone. He sat down softly and looked up into the trees, seeing many birds returning to their nests and hangout areas.

A couple of minutes passed, and his son could resist movement no longer. He funnelled his way out of the shrubbery with his hind leg limping. Once the birds began to chirp again, Wulfur would keep his eyes closed, thinking over the events of the last few hours.

"You can move now," Wulfur said, even though the adolescent pup had already grinded his way out of the flowery mess. The runt approached his father with his ears pulled back and eyes squinted.

"Well, that was a complete waste of time," he said with a solid tone. His voice was a bit boomy and snappy, with his dialect catching every letter allowing himself to be as clear as possible. He breathed heavily from his painful exhaustion.

"We convinced their leader to give us shelter. They were going to give us food. But instead, you infiltrated the main den immediately, fiddled with a pile of mice for a few hours, got caught doing it, then I got a piece of my ear bitten off and now here I am, hurt and starving. Brilliant plan, father."

As Wulfur listened to his son's view of the situation, his fangs slowly bared and his eyes veered open. Now hearing it mentioned, he hadn't noticed the chunk of ear missing from the pup. His guttery tone became even deeper, and his claws dug into the ground as he spoke.

"We knew the food was there, runt," responded the old timber male. "We didn't need to wait."

"You mean *you* didn't wait," the runt complained. "I didn't get any food."

"Well, that's tough," Wulfur pouted at his son, flicking his snout at the air. "You should have rallied up with me when I told you to. We're walking."

Wulfur got up and shook his pelt, discarding any loose pollen and bark that latched onto his fur. The runt had similar baring teeth with ripples of skin bumping his snout like ocean waves. He then, in turn, also shook his golden pelt, but with less vigour.

"Walking?" the runt shouted. "Are you kidding me? I'm exhausted!"

Reluctantly, the injured pup followed, hopping on three legs. He could feel pinches of twigs against his paws and loins, irritating him with every step. He followed behind his father who appeared to have way more energy and confidence despite what they had ran from.

"That's on you. Suck it up," Wulfur bellowed with his head turned slightly to the right, getting his son into peripheral view. "I've told you many times to pace yourself when you run. There's no point sprinting right away if the hunters look just like you. You keep doing that and someday you won't be running at all!" He noticed the size of his son decreasing in the corner of his eye. Wulfur stopped and turned to face him. "Are you even listening to me?"

He then watched his son raise his injured leg and mark his scent on the damp ground beneath him. The young golden male then kicked the dirt behind him with the other hind leg, spreading his urine scent across the narrow route and up one of the thinner trees. Wulfur gawped in disbelief.

"What are you doing? Do you want them to find us?!" Wulfur twitched an eyelid and lowered his head ominously. "There are scent glands in your paws too, foxbrain!"

His son sharply pointed his nose back at him, a stare so intimidating yet so fragile. He relaxed his legs and limped over with his tail poised outward. He confronted his father, approaching slowly with his ears hunched behind his head. Only exposing a few of his teeth, the runt kept a stable tone but only used his eyes to portray his level of seriousness.

"I know that, father," he said. "I did the same thing moments ago but a little further toward the North. I used my scent to lure those wolves away from us. I gave them a false trail to follow. That's why I was so far behind."

Wulfur eyed him, realising what he had done to deter the chasing group. His nostrils had stopped flaring and the ripples in his facial skin had calmed. The big male wolf let his tail dip lower, his posture casting a smaller shadow than before. He held his chin a bit higher as he looked down at his son. He had moved to within a wolf length of where he stood.

"Right, well... good." The timber male hesitated, not certain where to take his orders to next. "Just be more careful next time, runt."

The adolescent male tilted his head with puppy eyes as he looked up at his towering parent. His rear leg trembled in the background. Wulfur could now see his damaged ear. A small piece it was. He concluded that it would heal up enough to become hidden under new fur. He turned again and kept his head facing in his walking direction. His son caught up this time and walked alongside him.

"Father?" the runt asked softly. "When are you going to give me a real name?"

"Eh, runt will do for now," Wulfur replied.

"But if you say I was the only pup in the litter, then that name doesn't make sense," the runt contradicted, feeling sure he had that part right.

"The only surviving pup," Wulfur hesitantly reminded the runt.

"Whatever, I'm not little anymore," the youngster snapped, stiffening his shoulders. "And I don't want other wolves calling me that!"

Wulfur walked slower, allowing part of his mind to connect with his past. He knew the runt was indeed the only litter member without any stillborn or siblings to have died young. He did not want to tell the truth. He let his head dip slightly, his eyes softening. He peered over to his son who looked back at him closely as they trotted through the forest. Wulfur's voice became frail and reassuring.

"I'm sure we'll think of something, someday. But right now, we have a new place to explore. Listen to me carefully."

The runt was intrigued, his ears finally rising from their rest behind his head. Wulfur and his son took a route through the dark and narrow gaps between trees.

"We are heading South," Wulfur explained. "The woods will be more level, and we will need to cross a river. I could see it from the lookout ledge back at the den. And at the utmost South of this forest, there was black smoke. You know what that means, runt?"

The young male shook his head. Wulfur grunted under his breath before snickering at him.

"Humans. Or a human camp, probably."

Wulfur moved in front of his son to navigate through a tight gap between a pair of bushes teaming with blood red spikes. He marched in a straight line, feeling his fur coat scrape the surface of both the awkward bushes.

"Like the beings who fought the Greater Ones?" the runt asked, avoiding the stinging nettles by elegantly sliding between them, his rump and tail dancing on through.

"There's only a talon's worth. It's *the* Greater One, runt..." Wulfur tensed up all over, realising what his son had just said. That wasn't something he taught him about. He said '*Greater Ones*'. How did he find out?

Catching up to Wulfur's side once more, the runt let his ears lay the other way, so they pointed outward. He pulled his chin forward with his jaw and let his brows furrow slightly.

"No, no. I spoke to a few wolves in the pack. The Greater Ones are a coupapaw. Not just Ulfur. There was another called Likos, the rapscallion Blade, and um... I don't remember the last. But they were half a nest."

The forest around them creaked with the sound of wind through branches, but the air felt stale, like something had sealed it off. Wulfur let out a depressive sigh to fill the void. He knew the runt was right. The Greater Ones were indeed half a nest. He stood as strong as he made himself sound, not allowing the runt to sense him being in denial.

"They all knew about it," the runt continued. "They told me that you lied to me... You lied to me. Again. First about packs. Joining them being death wishes. And now the divines being just a lone talon?"

Wulfur squinted in anger at his son. The audacity he had to speak to him that way. He was his father. He wasn't going to stand for it, no matter how much the young wolf poked the hard truth in his face.

"Do you want me to start making you call me Wulfur again?" the old father growled. "Also, don't call them a pack. They just think they are. Their ranks, rituals, ceremonies. It's all bogus.

They're messed up. Why do you think I'm keeping you clear of them?"

His son hesitated, absorbing the change of topic and squeezing it dry with his desire to ask more questions. His head tilted a little more as they both tapped their paws over the flattening earth.

"Why is that your name anyway?" the runt wondered out loud. "Why does it sound a lot like Ulfur, the Greater One, wolf of might?"

The old father was going to snap a blood vessel. The anger ensued him until he quickly remembered who he was talking to. No fox, coyote or rogue wolf. It was the only wolf who trusted him right now. He let his eyes wander for a moment, using a passing butterfly as an excuse to consider his response.

"Rargh, Ravik!" Wulfur cursed lightly. His son clearly listened to too many stories from the roundup of wolves they had just evaded. "I told you before, my mother was forced to give me that name by Ulfur himself. It's a calling that I am to be the next great wolf god!" he explained, allowing his weight to shift from paw to paw. "By stealing the food and breaking the land, we'll make other wolves think I'm very powerful... I... *am* very powerful... when they hear my name, they'll bow before it."

"That doesn't make sense," the adolescent male noted.

Wulfur stopped and turned his head sharply toward his son, making physical contact with his snout. A series of inaudible sounds escaped Wulfur's breath before he was able to construct a confident reply to his persistent son.

"I think it does," he snarled through clenched teeth, his patience thinning. "And no other species of animal is getting it off easy either. I will... we will threaten the whole land!"

Wulfur's eyes were wide and full of gleaming light, guarded by jagged fur strands. He took a deep breath through his nose and spoke less aggressively.

"That point aside, we are going into that camp and taking as much food as we can carry in our mouths. Give us a head start, show them I'm a wolf to be afraid of!"

He started moving again, hoping that the golden wolf took a hint and knew that he wanted to focus on the journey ahead. But also, Wulfur needed to maintain his son's trust. Did he still trust him? The six-year-old timber wolf pondered the thought of having his own son at nine moons turn against him. What would he do?

He looked back at the runt and saw him staring blankly into the ground. Perhaps he was just being obedient. Their feet splodged through damp soil from the rain that had fallen earlier in the day. As Wulfur trudged along, he looked up to see the sun. It was going to go dark soon, and they would have to rest somewhere.

"Uh... father?" the young runt interrupted.

"What now?" Wulfur snapped.

"It's the ancestors," the runt replied, his voice reduced to a whisper.

Wulfur halted and turned around. His son was cowered like a submissive pup, looking half-way up a tree. His claws were fully extended, gripping the wet grass below him and his fur began to stand up on his neck and spine, like something was crawling under his skin.

Wulfur approached his son, observing the etched carving on the bark. It showed a rough image of two wolf heads facing each other with three claw marks encapsulating them. There was also a patch large enough to rest a wolf's plantar ball on and beneath that was a singular line placed next to a perfect dot.

Wulfur grunted as he turned to face the young male. His son appeared to be showing weakness... or even defiance? It didn't matter. He would crush it either way.

"You know the drill, runt. See the marking, head the other way. We're not dilly-dallying over your concerns, especially since you're questioning the count of ancestors with me. Ulfur wants me to rule these lands over both wolves and littler creatures. So that's exactly what I'm going to do!" he proudly beckoned, almost shouting his confidence at the poorly drawn symbol.

The runt shivered as he attempted to divert his eyes from the tree, taking notice of how leaves around it hadn't moved in the wind. They were motionless. Wulfur turned once more to the direction of the East and his son treaded carefully past the symbol, giving the tree extra breathing space.

"Weh- um... I'm sorry, father," he shamefully croaked. "I don't react quickly enough to it. It's unsettling. Like as if it's going to get me!" The feeling stuck with him, lurking inside his chest. He hated it.

The runt picked up the pace to move closer to Wulfur, who had stopped in front of yet another symbol, this time a couple of wavey lines etched in the dirt. Wulfur looked back at the runt. A slow burn accompanied his hazy stare. The father wolf could smell the runts' fear oozing out of him. With that, he tilted his head ever so slightly, his voice reaching a tone of mutual understanding.

"At least it's not the *real* spirit gate. You're with me and that means you are safe. You just need to be less lazy and help your old father out sometimes, hm?" Wulfur checked with the runt.

Another sense of undue hesitation filled the young wolf's head. He gave a cold stare at the shoulder of his father as he approached.

"Uh... yeah," he replied quietly.

"Come, now," Wulfur calmly chanted. "We should try to cross the river before it gets dark. Look at this." Wulfur stamped his paw above the etched image. "Water is nearby. A little way to go."

The golden wolf caught up and began to tail Wulfur, unable to shake the unease from his pelt. With his paws heavy, he took a brief peek over his shoulder to see if that symbol from the tree was following him. And then another. He huddled closer to his father, brushing against his fur, seeking the only comfort he knew. They disappeared into the abyss of trees, the whispers of the flowers engulfed by the wind.

Chapter 2

The golden wolf ploughed through the many rows of wild flora. He was far ahead of his father and was very eager to reach the river. Wulfur found it strange that his son had recovered from the leg injury so fast. He was dehydrated too, so maybe that is what kept him distracted from the pain in his leg.

"I smell borage, we must be close," the young wolf barked.

Wulfur watched his son joyfully lead the way toward the sound of flowing water. It was good to hear that his young runt had paid attention to where certain herbs could be found.

"Hey, slow it down. We got to remain vigilant!" he said, following the trail of disrupted plant life his son had jumped across.

"I know, I know. But you could be less uptight about me looking around," replied the golden male.

"I'm not uptight!" Wulfur stressed. "I just don't want to see you get into trouble again."

"Ah fine, di- whoa!"

The adolescent canine stopped in his tracks as he stared to the right of the opening at the rivers' edge. Wulfur wasn't as chipper, but still curious enough to wonder what his son had spotted. He brushed past the runt to see for himself, breaking the beech leaves with his paws.

He looked in the direction of interest and saw a plunge waterfall. Vertical walls of bedrock surrounded the multiple drops. Moss was growing on parts of the rock and a lot of trees covered up the view from the other side.

Above the waterfall itself was another majestic formation of rocks. The grey structures closed in on top of each other, blocking the view of the hills behind it and creating a hollow interior. This part really intrigued Wulfur. *'This could be some other wolf's den,'* he thought.

"It's beautiful. I get water first!" his son cried out as he shook his attention toward the tempting water in front of him and dashed toward it. He leant over with his tail wagging level with his body. He aimed his nose at the water and dipped it right in, lapping up the natural fluids he had so desperately needed.

"Yes... beautiful. A bit *too* beautiful to ignore..." Wulfur remarked, squinting his eyes at the sun. "Stay alert, runt. We might not be alone here."

"Mhmm, yeah, right," his son blabbed from under the water surface.

Wulfur felt sure something was off. How could any wolf looking for a place of rest come across this marvel of nature and think it wouldn't be worth claiming? He too approached the water and took a slow drink. He closed his eyes and kept his ears sharp, listening out for trouble.

The desperate young male slurped away at the rivers' edge. He then heard a light flap of wings to his left. The sound got loud quickly and then ceased. He felt something press on top of his spine. He paused with water still on his tongue and raised his head out to turn and see what had landed on him. It was a bird. It had black feathers and was rather small. The runt looked into the corvid's pea-sized eyes. It cawed at him. At first the golden male looked stunned, but then the crow made a move and flew toward a broken trunk nearer the fall. The runt stood up straight and trotted over to the crow, navigating around his father. Wulfur was still busy drinking up the water and thought nothing of his son taking a wander toward the rocks. He approached the crow and sniffed it from a few steps back.

"What are you up to?" he softly asked the crow. "You want me to follow you?"

The crow tilted its head, then plopped down to the ground and began hopping along the narrow path behind the waterfall. Its stick-thin legs made quick progress.

The runt hesitated for a moment, then followed, glancing back at his father, who had told him to be careful. Wulfur appeared too busy with the water to notice.

Behind the waterfall, the golden wolf observed the curved rock formation on his right. The crow stepped onto a rock across the way, which glinted with something shiny – more than just a metallic sheen. In some places, odd patches of colour shimmered, ranging from purple to blue, embedded in the surface.

The runts' eyes went wide with interest. He crept closer, gently pawing at the rock. The crow cawed again, fluttering off the rock as the runt went to touch it. The rock shifted slightly, revealing more of the embedded colour beneath. The runt pressed harder, digging with his claws into the bedrock. The material resisted, but his marks remained. Encouraged, he kept trying.

Suddenly, the crow let out a series of rapid caws, and the runt turned his head in time to see it fly out of the rocky shelter. Before he could react, a pair of massive black paws swooped over the golden wolf, pinning him by the shoulders.

The young wolf flinched and then felt the teeth of the entity grab his fur scruff within seconds. It growled above his head. He let out a loud yelp as his claws failed to grip in the rocks. His legs slid around until they left him helplessly lying down. He was terrified by the barrier of black fur blocking his view of the light.

Hearing the abrupt yelp from outside, Wulfur's hazel eyes flicked open, his tongue retreating from the water instantly. He let out a light gasp, seeing a black bird flee from behind the waterfall. His son was in danger! He bolted swiftly toward the narrow walkway, his paws just inches away from the rivers' edge.

Meanwhile, under the rock shelter, the runt made light attempts to free himself from the grip of the creature above him. The dark entity held onto him, not moving an inch, and the little wolf felt all hope drain out of his body, internally pleading for his father to rescue him.

"Stop moving..." it replied slowly. The male's voice was a deep whisper and had a small amount of mannerism to it. "It will only make the pain worse. Who are you and what are you doing in my shelter?"

The runts' lip trembled whilst his tail tried to curl under his collapsed body. "W...we were jus'... passing by. I...I don't have a name. Please!"

"No name?" he chuckled under his grip. "How will the ancestors be able to address you when your time is up?" His tone gradually increased in aggression as he shook the runts' pelt. His eyes were colourless, his fur coat an onyx black.

The golden wolf looked extremely confused and lost for what to say next. This was a question about the Greater Ones. He'd learned that they were half a nest only a day ago. He whined after hearing the black wolf speak of death into his ear. "Er... um... I don't know," he admitted shamefully.

"Hey!"

The mysterious wolf grunted, raising his brows to see the source of the interruption. There stood Wulfur, the wind tunnelling through his pelt with stray leaves curling up the rocky walls behind him. The runt also stopped moving but couldn't turn himself around to see his father.

"Let him go!" Wulfur commanded. The black wolf only let go of the runts' neck scruff so that he could speak clearly toward Wulfur. But he kept his paws firmly locked against the runts' shoulder blades and nose close to his neck.

The helpless golden wolf could feel the beast breathing over him. The fur between his shoulders tingled uncomfortably and caused him to whine.

"Father?" he whimpered, dragging his paws over his eyes.

The black wolf added up the clues around him. Then he gave a dark and menacing smirk toward Wulfur.

"You're the father? And you don't give the product of your own flesh and blood a name? The Greater Ones would be extremely disappointed."

Wulfur tried to limit his attention by looking at the eroded rock formations surrounding him. He wasn't going to let this stranger put him in the wrong.

"Did you hear what I said? Get off him! Who do you think you are?"

"I am known as the Wise Wolf," the dark wolf said with a level tone. "My real name is obsolete to the neighbouring territories, but at least I got mine at birth."

Wulfur curled his paws at the ground, slowly sharpening his claws as he did so. His right eye twitched and his front teeth exposed under his nose, seeing the Wise Wolf give him a deadpan stare in return. Was this an attempt to mock him of how he raised his son?

"Don't play omega-fool with me, cave dweller," Wulfur growled, his patience crumbling beneath his paws. "A wise wolf wouldn't dare challenge me. When you learn who I am, then you'll be sorry."

The Wise Wolf's grip lessened over the shoulders of the runt. His face calmed but remained slightly unnerving. He slowly raised his head so he could see more level with his listener.

"I know who you are, Wulfur," the Wise Wolf disclosed.

Wulfur let out a sharp growl, his exterior proving unintimidated by the sudden revelation of the Wise Wolf's knowledge. Wulfur's mission involved making all wolves fear him by name, but he had barely done anything yet to boost that reputation. To be known by name from a stranger felt unusual. He knew it was what he wanted, but in this situation, it did not make sense.

The Wise Wolf continued. "I know you steal food from stronghold dens." The runt twitched his body beneath him, the Wise Wolf pressing on him hard in response. "You bury your teeth into blood of your own kind in honour of a divine you can't become."

"You know nothing about me!" Wulfur snapped back. "Now let him go or die."

The Wise Wolf looked between Wulfur and the runt, weighing his decision. He saw the frightened young wolf's body language. He seemed innocent enough to spare. If it were the other way around, he doubted there would be much time to talk before a fight began. Wulfur spread his legs slightly, taking a wide stance, covering the exit.

As fierce as he appeared, the Wise Wolf did not have any plans to hurt the little pup. He had positive morals, but he would hide them from these strangers intruding his den.

The Wise Wolf took a paw off the runt and used the other to budge him away. The runt scrambled to his feet and fled for cover under his muscular father. The Wise Wolf turned his head for a moment, feeling at ease by his decision.

In that second, Wulfur broke his son's cover and charged at the Wise Wolf, eyes scrunched and jaw wide open, revealing the frightening scale of his teeth. In reaction to Wulfur's advance, the Wise Wolf's eyes narrowed briefly and let his jaw gawp for a second before baring his fangs back at him.

The runt watched the pair collide, the initial shock from the bite still making him wobble. Wulfur pummelled into the Wise Wolf, his teeth puncturing the skin beneath the cheek fur. The Wise

Wolf snarled briefly as he tried to drag his head past Wulfur's and go for the side of his neck. They both failed to get a solid grip and backed away from each other. The Wise Wolf tried to start circling around him, but Wulfur didn't move, blocking his way past and not being able to target a weak spot.

"You broke our deal," the Wise Wolf preached. "Your son is free and you're trying to kill me."

"Maybe if you were wise, you wouldn't have trapped him in the first place," Wulfur argued back cockily.

They snarled at each other. Wulfur's teeth were red, unlike the Wise Wolf, who hadn't tasted his blood yet. Wulfur's bite had left him with a small rip on his cheek which bled gently down his jaw. Both of their backs arched upward. The Wise Wolf could understand what Wulfur was trying to say. But this level of betrayal was intolerable.

Then they both heard a faint squeak from the opening.

"Father, let's just go."

Wulfur briefly looked over to frown at his son.

The Wise Wolf saw his chance and leapt at Wulfur whilst his head was turned. Wulfur's back thudded against the rocky ground after he was tackled, feeling the skull of his opponent punch him in the chest. He stretched his paws upward to push against the shoulders of the Wise Wolf, his jaws now aiming for his throat.

"Father!" his son cried, seeing the timber wolf collapse, becoming interlocked with the black beast.

Wulfur leaned his head upside down to see a distorted view of his son. He spoke with grunts between words as the Wise Wolf tried to shake his neck loose from his paws.

"Don't just stand there, runt. Help me tear this pile of fox faeces apart!"

The Wise Wolf spat in Wulfur's face as he spoke, now more aggressive in tone.

"Your boy is right. You should have just walked away. If you keep trying to fight, I will make sure there's nothing left of you to bury!" His claws were starting to draw blood from Wulfur's brisket and fore chest. Wulfur made slow grunts, trying to suppress the receptive signals of pain with anger.

"Runt, I said help me!" he looked away from his son to see the Wise Wolf wrap his fangs around his right pastern and chew hard. His front legs stiffened upwards, resisting submission or a clean strike at his neck. His body wriggled violently as the pair exchanged barks and snarls.

They both started kicking at each other's underbellies with their hind legs, leaving many scratches and bruises in their wake. Wulfur let off his guard by missing a jump upward with his jaws at the other's face. The Wise Wolf took advantage and stamped his claws into Wulfur's flank, making him yelp. A light cackle escaped the Wise Wolf's maw from the satisfaction of hitting Wulfur where it hurt.

The young wolf didn't obey his father's orders. He just watched in terror. His heart sunk whilst his legs went frail. Then he spoke pleadingly over the sound of gushing water close by.

"Please, Wise Wolf. Don't kill him."

The thought of living without his father made his heart pound. He knew he'd be completely lost without him.

"He's my father," the runt cried, reminding the Wise Wolf of what he was allowing the young wolf to witness. Wulfur had been beaten, and the Wise Wolf could see his limbs becoming weak. He would easily be able to slice his throat soon... but he stopped.

Hearing the runts' pleading words, he pushed all his paws into Wulfur, giving him an extra hit to his guts before propelling off him. Wulfur snarled at the Wise Wolf from where he laid and awkwardly rolled over onto his belly.

The Wise Wolf returned to the spot where he had been knocked into earlier and tucked his head into his chest.

"It's a shame that boy is with you," he said, shuffling his tail out of view. "If he were less delusional, he would have let me kill you."

Wulfur rose to his feet in an embarrassing struggle. His withers were raised, and his tail was upright.

"Stop it! Shut your maw!" His voice was so boomy it echoed under the waterfall. He then turned his neck toward his son and gave him a cold stare with fangs on display. "We're going," he announced in monotone.

The runts' tail was so far curled it covered his sheath. His hocks wobbled as he looked back into the eyes of the wolf who he had convinced to spare his father.

The Wise Wolf watched as Wulfur limped his way toward the clearing in front of the fall. He scoffed quietly, then looked at the young wolf who had his back turned away from him.

"You were very brave to interfere for that wretch of a father," the Wise Wolf said. "You should try lying to *him* once in a while."

The runts' ears perked up followed by a slight turn of his head, bringing the sight of the Wise Wolf into the corner of his eye.

"Give it time and you will find that you won't need him anymore," the Wise Wolf finished before turning his head away, pretending to admire the rocky walls. Then he began to lick the base of his paws, tasting Wulfur's blood and a bit of his own.

The young male tried to ignore the Wise Wolf as he took a long look at his limping father. He had barely survived. The Wise Wolf's words echoed in the walls of the cave and began to circle his ears. With only the sound of the waterfall to cover up his shaky breathing, the runt remained stunned, and saliva dripped out of his mouth. But then the lack of comfort evoked fear into the runt. Realising his father had left without him, he sprinted out of the rock shelter without looking back.

Outside, the day had grown old. The sky was pink, and the grasshoppers could be heard chirping near the river's edge. The water that moved gently downstream after passing the drop reflected the orange sun and the inhabitants that walked by it. Wulfur and his son were a part of it. They were a long way down the river, looking for a safe place to cross. Wulfur paid extra attention to the shallow parts, whilst his son trotted behind, observing the grassy terrain he walked on.

The older timber wolf winced as he was being reminded of the many scars he obtained in his battle with the Wise Wolf. Who was he, and where did he come from? More importantly... how did he know his name?

Both wolves navigated single file across a stretch of water, shallow enough to only engulf their paws. From high up a tree, the crow that had guided the runt into danger watched them as they crossed. It took to the skies and followed them into the woods.

They entered an area of broken trees and a lot of open space. Wulfur didn't feel as confident seeing so much exposure of the flat land. The thought of bears roaming wildly and snakes hiding beneath the ground. It was concerning enough for Wulfur to momentarily consider turning back.

The golden wolf saw the scenery and noticed that a lot of tree trunks had been severed. The open air was very bizarre to feel as they stood in what should be deep forest.

"We'll rest here," Wulfur finally decided, the quietness of the woods being an inviting experience. Apart from being with his son, it would be pure solitude.

It was windy and barely a creek could be heard from the surrounding woods. As the night pressed on, the pair relaxed against a surviving tree with only the light of the crescent moon beaming down at them. A mighty sequence of howls could be faintly heard in the wind, breaking the illusion that they were alone.

"I wonder what happened to all the trees," his son pointed out, knowing this wasn't a natural occurrence. "Father, there's some goldenrod on that shrub over there. I can get it for you to help sooth your wounds."

Wulfur laid there and didn't move, nor look at his son.

"No thanks," he replied with a cold expression.

The runt got up and approached his father whilst he chewed on some poppy seeds. "There were a few meadows back there with some of these great stress relievers," he reported, crunching away. He paused his chewing when he saw his father's head stiff like a stone. "What's wrong?" the runt asked.

"You, mostly," his father replied, shifting the weight between his paws.

The runt gawped. "Me? I'm trying to help you."

"Yes, but back there, you refused to fight," said Wulfur. His voice became groggy, almost sounding too lazy to talk.

"I was injured and hungry," the runt complained back, accidentally spitting a few seeds in Wulfur's direction. "Besides, I still saved you."

"Irrelevant!" Wulfur barked at his son, aggressively wiping his face of the few seeds that had hit him. "If you had attacked him with me, that pretty waterfall could have been ours! Not every wolf has a sense of compassion. Your mother didn't."

This tangent halted their discussion for a moment. Wulfur thought about his mate who had birthed his boy. He sighed with a lump in his throat.

"Evelyn."

"You speak of my mother's name a lot," the runt said, moving up close to his father before slowly planting his bottom on the ground. "But is that why she's not here? What did she do?"

Wulfur hesitated and rubbed his paws hard into the dirt. Leaning his head down, he met his son's unique golden eyes. They were the same as hers. This made Wulfur lower the steam from his head. He cleared his throat and began to explain.

"Our pack..." Wulfur paused, realising he described his home as a pack. He faked a gag, making sure the runt knew that calling it a pack was wrong. "The wolves were jealous of our superiority. Me and your mother decided to rebel after mating. She was pregnant with you whilst I burnt down the stronghold."

The runt raised a paw off the ground, close to Wulfur's nose.

"Wait, you used fire?" he questioned. "How?"

"You don't need to know," Wulfur replied sternly.

"Only the humans can create fire," the runt reminded him.

"Don't worry about it, runt. Just assume I had their power." Wulfur wavered his snout, hinting to his son that he no longer wanted that paw in his face.

The runt acknowledged this and moved his paw back down next to the others. He let his thighs rest against the ground, allowing his whole body to slump to one side. His front paws consumed his weight as he kept an intrigued glance at his father.

"Okay...? So, *then* what happened?"

"We uh... ran off together..." Wulfur said as his front paws began to clench the dirt. "...and I thought we were going to become what I believed we'd be: the most feared wolves in the forest. We would have raised a strong family and had been untouchable. But... after you were born, she... just left."

"Why?" the runt asked abruptly.

"She just did," Wulfur replied. "No explanation. Just disappeared."

The runt tilted his head in confusion. "Why didn't you try to find her?"

Wulfur kept eye contact with his son. He saw some flashbacks entering his mind. As he relived these thoughts, his eyes would slowly drift toward the ground.

Mating with Evelyn was the first of those to infiltrate his mind. He could hear their discussion as he had been holding himself against her.

"You're on omega, my love. If the pack finds out, the Alpha will tear your insides out," she had said.

"And when they do, we can run together," Wulfur replied.

"I can't just run away from the pack. I'm a plains wolf with yellow fur. The Alpha wants my pups," Evelyn argued back.

"Well, I promise that I'll bring you the strongest most healthy litter of puppies you could imagine for!" Wulfur proposed, his paws holding her tighter. "Not a pack, but a mighty band of Minnesota Plains hybrids! It is our destiny."

"You believe so?" she wondered. She stared hard into the open, feeling Wulfur's physical rhythm and words entice her into submission, sealing her bond further.

"I know so," declared Wulfur. "It's what the ancestors foretold."

The sound of the lustful panting faded away as the next thought was that of the Alpha banishing Evelyn in front of the entire pack. Wulfur had been hiding behind a lavender bush listening in from a few hundred feet away. The situation was a huge blow to Evelyn, but Wulfur had confidence in his destiny.

The voice of the Alpha could be heard. "You have disgraced our pack by plaguing the strength of future generations. The Greater Ones are furious with me that I didn't stop you in time. Begone,

Evelyn. And never return, unless you want your young to be tormented as omegas for eternity."

The Alpha watched Evelyn turn and leave without another word. Then he walked up to a hunter. "If you ever catch that ugly swine Wulfur, I want his head on my council rock."

The sight of woeful wolves from the pack faded as the next flashback took hold. It was after the pup was born. Very soon after. They were miles away from the pack grounds. Wulfur had been towering over Evelyn as she bled turmoil from her eyes.

"Maybe there's another coming," Wulfur withered, analysing Evelyn's belly for other bumps.

"There isn't, Wulfur. That's it." Evelyn gave Wulfur a disgusted look as she attempted to bat him away from her body with a paw. "Blade's deceit, what have I done? What have you done?"

"Evelyn, you need to calm," Wulfur begged, his undertone exposing some fragility under his big ego.

"Why should I?!" she bellowed and got up aggressively, feeling the latch of the pup to her teat break loose. "This pup is terribly ill as well. I want to scream. You're nothing but a filthy delusional paw-pack lowlife wretch! You were in the omega ranks for a reason and I should never have thought otherwise! Traitor to the pack, traitor to me!"

"B-but...the, the pup..." Wulfur gawped at Evelyn's shock move that caused the pup to collapse helplessly on the ground. His eyebrows and ears inched further apart as he watched his mate stand defensively against him.

"You know what? I don't even care. He's your problem now. You promised me healthy pups and... urgh I feel so stupid. Don't try to follow me," she bellowed in sorrow as she sprinted into the woods.

"No Evelyn, wait!" He got up to go chase her with plead in his eyes. The worry turned into dread as he watched his mate disappear into the darkness, never to return.

"Father?" A sudden light male voice spooked Wulfur as he looked back at the sick pup. Its whining made him panic in thought.

"Father?!" the runt called, seeing him stare aimlessly into the night. Finally, Wulfur snapped out of his daydream and refocused his son, once again seeing the same eyes as Evelyn. The question he hadn't answered yet. What was it? His son looked at him with much intrigue.

"Hm?" Wulfur asked back.

"Why didn't you go after her?" his son repeated, swallowing the last poppy seed.

"I guess her love for me made me weak," Wulfur said, his tone a little softer than normal. "If you...fall in love with a wolf, they are useable against you. I was better off without her anyway... it is likely she thought the same about me."

Wulfur rested his chin in the dirt that he excavated with his paws. The young male slouched a bit before laying down next to his father. He licked his lips clean, then snorted to clear the pollen from his nose. He then laid on his side, with his front paws flailing playfully.

"So, what does love actually feel like?" he asked as he rubbed the side of his face into the ground, searching for the best spot to rest his head.

Wulfur stretched his front legs as he spoke with a relieving strain in his voice.

"Yeah, it's probably best that you don't know. That way you can always remain strong. Focus on surviving. Make less mistakes at the expense of others. Love does feel good, I'll tell you that, runt. But it's not worth the heartbreak."

Wulfur closed his eyes and tried to listen to the crickets of the night. His son fidgeted as he tried to lean his head past his own shoulder. He sighed in annoyance and looked over at Wulfur.

"Euh... father?"

"What do you want?" Wulfur quietly croaked.

"I've got an itch on my scruff, and I can't get to it." The runt attempted to point at the spot with his nose.

"Ignore it," Wulfur said with no hesitation.

The silence went on for a while and it was not normal. Wulfur opened his eyes to see his son staring at him with his lower jaw pronounced forward. The brows looked sad sat upon the runts' puppy eyes and his paws were lifeless. Wulfur knew what he wanted. "Alright, come on then."

His son's expression changed wildly. The runts' eyes widened with joy, his tail wagged playfully, his fangs trying to break through a smile. The runt rolled over so that his back was pressed against Wulfur's belly. Wulfur leaned his head up to bring his nose toward the runts' neck scruff. He then began to groom the fur, licking and teething at the middle spot.

The runt closed his eyes and gently laid his head back down on its side.

"Up a bit, up a bit. Yeah… that's it, that's the spot," the golden wolf quietly cooed. The feeling of his father's tongue sent a calming tingle through his body. That along with the feeling of protection where his spine met Wulfur's warm underbelly.

Wulfur slowed his grooming pace, remembering how much his son asked for this as a pup. He felt his own breathing slow down too as the runt fell asleep under his chin. *'He likes to have this after he gets hurt,'* Wulfur thought to himself. *'He doesn't want me to clean his wounds. Just wants the neck licked. Must be quite relaxing for him.'*

Tomorrow would be an important day for them: a chance to see the human camp up close and Wulfur wanted the smoothest operation possible. *'Humans, hm…'* Wulfur pondered. *'Didn't think I'd encounter them again.'* He thought of the possibility that the camp would disband before they reached it. Would the humans be preparing for a battle with the Greater Ones? Or were they survivors of it? On that thought, Wulfur dozed off, letting his exposed forepaw rest over the sleeping runts' shoulders.

Chapter 3

Bright sunshine cast over the broken woods. Wulfur and his son were on the hunt for some food. Infiltrating the human camp would surely require energy, and right now they were low on it. Critically, his son hadn't tasted meat in a few days. Seeing how much of the forest had vanished, Wulfur knew the young golden male wouldn't last long on herbs. Wulfur took an inhale of the air. His nasal senses registered the odour from the smoke of the place they were headed to. They were much closer now, but this meant they needed a meaty meal quickly. He placed his nose on the ground to try and pick up a trail. There was a trace of white-tail deer.

"Bless the divines," he muttered. "Runt! Over here. I found a trail, but it's weak. I'll move down the hill into that coup – see if it's hiding there. You go the other way, see if it's in that glade over there. Be slow – don't spook it. If you get the chance, take it. I'll be close enough after I hear the commotion. You do the same for me, got it?"

He listened and nodded every time Wulfur paused for breath.

"Yes, father," he acknowledged, him too knowing it was this or nothing for food.

"Good." Wulfur bounced his paws up to get some flexibility into his joints and began to tiptoe toward the coup of trees. He stopped to ponder for a moment. *'Why did these trees grow unharmed, but those across the North dead and missing?'* Quickly shifting his focus to his hunger, he continued down the hill.

Meanwhile, the runt began to lightly pad his way to the clearing of long grass and dandelions. He didn't feel prepared to lash out at a deer. The thought of his father's disappointment was somewhat expected but sad too. There was a cawing sound from above. The golden wolf looked up to see a crow soaring above him. It began to descend until it placed itself on a strange log. This piece of wood was incredibly smooth, stood upright and had a rounded top with no branches. The golden wolf paid more attention to the crow that stood atop the bizarre wood piece. He looked at the crows' head movements and widened his eyes.

"You. You're the corvid who got me in trouble with that wolf by the river. Why did you do that?"

The runt couldn't be sure it understood him or spoke wolf. The crow simply squawked back at him and rapidly shook its wings clean. It made another caw before flying off toward the glade. The young wolf grumbled as his ears tucked into his head. Smelling the air, he tried to pick up on where the crow was headed. But then, he caught an even stronger scent through his nose. It was a stench so foul that the runt had to tighten his lips to prevent coughing. The crow he watched had flown towards it. His adventurous mind encouraged him to go and check it out. He figured that if something smelt this awful, it couldn't be dangerous.

The runt lowered himself and crept through the tall grass to then peer through the clearing. It was an unbelievable sight. It was the white-tailed deer dead on the ground, being pecked by a nest of crows. He gasped and held his jaw low. He observed, smelled and listened to his surroundings. There didn't appear to be any sign as to what killed it.

Picking up on nothing else, he withdrew from his cover and approached the deer. Every corvid apart from the familiar one instantly flew off. The runts' nose was going crazy as he examined the corpse. He looked up at the solitary crow that perched on the deer's antlers.

"Oh, is this what you were trying to show me?"

Knowing that no answer was coming, his attention quickly locked onto the carcass. The stench flooded his nostrils whilst his mouth watered at the spongey belly of this dead animal.

"Runt! What did you...?"

The golden male jolted from hearing his nickname, and the last crow took to the skies as Wulfur emerged from the thicket of grass. He could see his son standing over a fresh deer corpse with no other animal scent around.

"Did you kill it all by yourself?" Wulfur asked, analysing the corpse from behind the runt.

The young wolf stared lifelessly at his father, vaguely remembering the words of the Wise Wolf from yesterday. Should he try lying to him? The runt was curious to see how dishonesty would change his fathers' response. He let his jaw wander with his golden eyes, thinking of the best thing to say.

"Yes," he finally replied.

Wulfur bopped his head a little way behind his chest in surprise. He came up to the deer and looked over its wounds. The runt knew that those in place were peck marks from the crows. However, Wulfur also spotted the trail of blood made by the deer. It veered off into nowhere and he felt too hungry to worry about it.

"Right, well... er... nice work, runt," said Wulfur, casting a little grin at him. "Keep this up and I might call you Hunter."

The praise felt unusual for the runt. He hadn't seen his father this proud of him. Ever.

"Thanks. And no... that name sucks," the runt commented, poking his tongue out.

"Eat up, runt," Wulfur said eagerly. "We can't waste this."

Without another moment's hesitation, Wulfur dug his fangs into the belly of the deer. His son walked around the other side to munch on the neck. He saw a small circular hole in the flesh across the neck and began to chomp through there. They both chowed on some much-needed protein. But right at the point of pure feeding satisfaction, the runt bit into an extremely hard object, sending a great amount of pain through his gums and upper jaw. He yelped loudly and stepped away from the carcass. Wulfur looked up, surprised. Half his snout was stained in blood.

"Did you crunch a bone or something? They're not that hard to chew." He resumed eating. His son, now feeling dizzy, spat out the deer blood as he could taste something strange.

"Yeah, I think I did. It was just a bit unexpe-" The young wolf froze as he spotted the object that he chewed. He moved his nose closer to the dirt. It resembled a small cylinder with a broken end to it. It felt harder than wood, but what interested the runt mostly was the colour. Yellow but metallic and shiny.

He thought for a moment whilst taking in its bizarre but striking shape. *'The crow had shown me a shiny object before. Maybe it wasn't the food he drew me toward after all.'* It would explain why no other scent was around, and the only explanation for the deer's... death.

'Uh oh,' he thought, quickly splitting a gap between his paw pads to grip the metal object in between. He quickly stuffed it in his ear. If his father saw this, he would know that he lied. The object was unmistakable due to its' size and shine, but given it was a similar colour to his ear lobe, he hoped his father wouldn't notice. He came back quickly and began chewing at the rear of the carcass, trying to distract himself.

Wulfur looked up again. At first, he was going to question the nature of his sudden halt on words. But seeing his son chowing down on the deer's bottom kept him amused and without a reason to be suspicious. He chuckled with a mouth full of liver and dove his snout in again.

The runt sat up to take a breath between dives into the gory mess. His head appeared over the tall grass to observe around and saw many rows of greenery far and wide. This didn't appear to a be a particularly small clearing. He licked his snout, which was stained red from the fresh meat, when something caught the corner of his eye.

He saw what looked like a square tree amongst the distant bushes. It had a gap shaped like a letterbox and from that opening came a bright twinkle of light... and it moved. His eyes widened with fascination, the flash reflecting against his retina like an exploding star.

"Whoa, father. What's that?"

Wulfur knew that if the runt was curious, he could get into trouble. Reluctantly, he removed his face from the belly of the deer and sat up too to see what the disruption was. When the glint of light in the distance hit his eye, Wulfur immediately dropped the food out of his mouth and his ears darted to the sides of his head. His breathing became jolty, and then rapid as he whipped his whole body away from the light. His paws scampered in the dirt, sliding over the bloody mess from the corpse.

"RUN! RUN NOW!" he bellowed at the top of his lungs.

Unaware of the reasons, the golden male scampered onto his feet and chased Wulfur back up the hill. Then they both heard a sudden, deafening sound. It popped in their eardrums, startling the runt. Wulfur felt the pulse of the air as a hot light shot past them both, clearing his head by centimetres. He ducked instinctively, attempting to avoid the shot. All the birds hiding in the trees took flight and filled the sky, causing Wulfur to misplace his paws whilst running.

The runt stopped moving from the sound shock, and Wulfur noticed this. As his father spoke, the runt could barely understand what he was saying. He felt his ears ringing which only fuelled his confusion. Unlike Wulfur, the young male chose to hold his breath, standing stiff as a stone, wanting the pain in his ears to stop.

"Come on, we need to sprint away. It's going to kill us!" his father's words coming out in a muffled mess.

Panicked, the runt struggled to speak, but he recognised Wulfur's body signals as a way of saying "let's go". Nodding, he resumed running and led the way this time instead of Wulfur. The golden wolf's tail was tucked under whilst Wulfur's held out behind him, flailing in the wind. The older timber wolf looked ahead of his son and saw the route through to safety.

"Over there, runt, down into the coup. Hurry!"

As they got closer, Wulfur felt the ground become uneven. He knew their survival will depend on how quickly they could evade the line of sight from the threat. The trees on the slope of land ahead had their leaves hanging close to ground level with some tall grass for good measure.

His son slithered through the grass whilst Wulfur jumped between the varied forage in as open space as he could. Both wolves collapsed on the ground and Wulfur tucked his head close to his son's. He could feel him breathing slow but heavily. Wulfur attempted to keep his respiration patterns the same whilst his eyes were wide with adrenaline.

"We'll be safe here. That was a human. With their 'black magic' contraption."

"B-b... black magic?" the runt withered, panting excessively in the warm air.

"It's something they hold when hunting," Wulfur explained, pressing his chin on the runts' stiff body. "They point it at whatever they want dead, and after the bang, it's dead... instantly. Maybe they harness power from the skies, I don't know. But it- wait. What's that in your ear?"

Wulfur sat up within the dark shrubbery overlay and investigated him. The runt took a moment to catch on due to his ringing eardrums and heavy breathing. Quickly he realised that Wulfur had seen the shiny object in his left lobe.

Before he could even speak, Wulfur padded him behind the scalp and knocked the metallic object to the earth. Wulfur's eyes widened as he noticed its lack of bloodstain and looked toward his son.

"Where'd you find this?" he asked with a serious glare.

"Oh just... around," the golden wolf replied nervously.

Wulfur blinked and tucked his brows closer together. "When?"

"I've had it a long time," the runt falsely stated. "I just don't normally store it in my ear."

The young male knew how silly it sounded, but he hoped that Wulfur would believe him as the object smelled like the interior of his ear. Wulfur pinched the object and held it between his digits in confusion. He licked the blood stains off his snout whilst he observed it.

"Wha- where else would you store it?" Wulfur asked his son, his eyes scanning over his body for anything else that could be hiding. "Behind your teeth? Up your tailhole?"

The golden male shifted his legs from where he sat and curled his tail. He didn't want his father to know that he hadn't killed the deer. He nodded with a light hum from his mouth. Wulfur twitched an eye in disgust, but then calmed as the thought of self-sufficiency silenced any doubts he had.

"Urgh, I suppose that's what the Greater Ones *could* have done to deliver all those medicines to our predecessors. But why would you keep something like this? Do you even know what this is?"

His son shrugged. "It's shiny, I know *that* much."

Wulfur frowned and held his head below his shoulders, tossing the metallic cylinder into the wilderness. The runt watched in unpleasant surprise as he lost sight of his shiny find.

"That, runt, was a product of the black magic. Wherever you found it, a sub-god had summoned it to kill an animal. Don't try to think about it too much. It drives some wolves insane. Let's move this way. It looks safer."

Wulfur set off through the maze of shrubs. Much to the runts' disappointment, his father might have been right this time. These humans did indeed hold a bewildering power. Were they ever to know how it worked?

Then he thought back to the crow again. Shiny rocks behind the waterfall, the metallic cylinder-flower. He knew that corvids were naturally smart. Either this crow had been guiding him to things that fascinated him... or to places of danger just for fun. That latter thought put a chill down his spine. Right now, he could not trust the crow. On both occasions of following it, he had near misses with death. He gulped at his closing thought and trotted after his father, keeping these theories along with his feelings to himself.

As the afternoon settled in, Wulfur had led the way to the east side of the black smoke where the forest grounds had been richer in plant life. Now striding toward the source, he slowed and leaned his head through each curve of shrubbery, just in case he was closer than he expected. There was no need to infiltrate now. Daylight made them easier to spot.

The smell of burning was now rich. His sensitive, wet nose took in a lot of information about the camp as they closed in. There was the smell of salmon, hog and most obviously of all, humans. Wulfur's ears perked up as his paws came to a standstill. He looked behind his shoulder, seeing his son trailing behind with his head pointed to the ground.

"Shh! I think we're here," Wulfur said with a hint of optimism. "But we're not going in right away. Wait here, runt. I'm going to check it out."

"Be careful, father," the runt whispered back with an upset tone.

Wulfur rotated his head briefly to move on in but halted again after hearing his son speak. He turned to him and came close. The runt sat down as he saw his father bring his right paw up to his face. The young wolf gasped. Wulfur paused his movements. He gave his son a somewhat caring look in the eyes and then began to slowly place his paw behind his son's head. He spoke calmer than he had done in a while. Wulfur then ruffled the back of the runts' damaged ear in sympathy.

"You have no reason to worry about me," Wulfur assured the runt. "After today, we are going to be loaded with food. Think about that. I know you're down. Confused. Maybe sad, even. But this is my calling. You only need to help me when I ask for it. It's my destiny I need to fulfil. Maybe after I'm gone... you'll find yours."

The young male looked up at his father's caring stare as he spoke of the future. Just like the Wise Wolf had done, Wulfur put the thought of living alone in his mind. It was unimaginable to the runt.

"You're saying I'll find a way?" he asked his father. "Even without you?"

"Yes," Wulfur bluntly replied.

"But how can I believe you?" The runts' voice raised, a lump beginning to form in the back of his throat. "After all the lies you told me, why should I take any of this for granted? Is it possible that I can't survive by myself? Tell me."

The surrounding environment became eerily quiet. As Wulfur struggled to comprehend such an open question, he felt a cold but familiar presence in the wind. It felt like whispers were transmitting through his body.

Closing his eyes for a moment, he allowed these voices to dance atop him. He silently dipped his head. *'Ancestors help me. What do I tell him?'* Wulfur sighed knowing the answer would only come at the ancestral spirit gate they passed yesterday. He slowly opened his eyes and spoke in a grumpy tone once more.

"Look. A wolf tells lies to get what they want. I lied to the wolves in my home so that I could be with your mother. With that, I got respect and control. It's the reason you exist."

With that, Wulfur shook his son's head a little harder and then let go. He leaned forward and bopped the side of his snout with the tip of his tongue. At that moment, he froze. He met the runts' gaze and felt the ambient pressure of giving his son affection during his loss of confidence. Then he turned and headed through the thicket of bushes without another word.

The golden male put his own paw carefully on where his father licked him. Still sat where he had been listening, the runt took a moment to process what his father had just said. Hearing the last of his fathers' footsteps fade, the golden wolf's head faced downward so that he could focus on his own paws. They fidgeted and his claws parried in response. As he was deep in thought, he let out a regretful sigh. The wind blew through his chest, parting the fur from under his brisket. He closed his eyes as he tried to imagine life without his father.

Meanwhile, Wulfur pitter-pattered his way through a row of alders. From the flurry of purple needlegrass that wavered between them, Wulfur peeked over and saw the immense complexity of the human camp. It was a steep drop before him to get onto the flattened soil that the humans had created to build the camp on. The first thing that caught his attention was a tall post with a waving flag that was labelled 'Natural Resource Extraction Agency'.

To the right of that was a ginormous stack of tree trunks. Wulfur thought for a moment, then connected the dots. It was the humans that had removed the trees from the broken woods. They might have kept these trees nearby still standing to hide their camp from the Greater Ones.

He then observed the large structure that a couple of men walked into. It appeared to be the same texture as the logs. Wulfur could see that their trees were being used to build shelters. Attached to the structure was a moderately sized metal contraption, making a lot of noise. Behind the noisemaker was a grey and white spire that pointed high into the sky with a light glimmering at the top. This light was red, but his wolf eyes were only able to process white.

Further right of the cabin, Wulfur could see the superweapon of humanity, engulfing wood inside a sacred circle of rocks. Fire. He knew that fire was incredibly dangerous but was myth-boggled by how they were able to contain it so well.

Looking more around that area, he could see big, sand-coloured crates. Surely, they contained food. A pair of humans were lifting a crate toward the cabin. They placed it just before the entrance and they turned to see another human emerge from the far side. He was holding a long stick that combined wood and metal. Wulfur suspected this was the hunter who had attempted to kill him.

He could see the pair of men speaking with each other, but he didn't understand the human tongue. *'He's probably telling them about us!'* he thought. Wulfur wasn't going to be phased by their awareness of wolves roaming the land. It was likely him and the runt were among many wolves in the region. There had been no stories to suggest that wolves were extinct across the land.

With that hiccup out of the way, Wulfur looked past the cabin and saw what looked like sitting places made from more wood. Further on was a small but strangely shaped structure with a human resting over the side of it. The larger wooden stilts connected to a hexagonal roof, curving upward to a point at the top. Nature couldn't ever form something like that.

Left of that was a bizarre stone carving, with a hollow interior. Attached to the top of it by rope was a few other light wooden objects filled with water. Wulfur dragged his eyes back to where he started. There was a row of smaller shelters to the left of the grey contraption. Their entrances appeared to flap in the wind whilst being held in place with sticks in the ground. Maybe they stored food in there too.

It was then that Wulfur heard a loud rumbling sound. He ducked his head into the needlegrass and tried to identify where it came from. It was getting louder. He could see the men approach the far-left side and lift a white metal barrier. Then, from the large pathway, came a humungous machine moving on what appeared to be rotating cylinders. The land vessel slowed and crept loudly across the camp.

Wulfur could hear the humans shouting at the machine as it weaved between the supply crates and came to a standstill by the pile of logs. He watched as the humans worked together to drag the dead trees one-by-one onto the back of it. Wulfur could see a human faintly inside the front checking around himself before shouting back at the others. Wulfur decided he had seen enough and scurried away. The humans finished loading the last log, then they tapped on the land vessel, signalling it to go.

Wulfur returned to where he had asked his son to wait and looked around. There was no sign of him, yet he could smell that he hadn't gone far.

"Runt?" he called out.

"Up here," whispered a familiar voice.

The older wolf's ears went erect, and he leaned his head backward. He saw a familiar golden tail dangling over a tree branch.

"What in holly berries are you doing up there?!"

His son was hunched against the trunk and had left enough room to lay across the oak branch. He peered down to see Wulfur looking slightly unimpressed.

"I'm practicing a new survival tactic," the runt said proudly.

"What? By embracing your inner jaguar? You'll injure yourself! Get down here. I got much to discuss."

As the golden wolf nodded, he attempted to shift his way down. But suddenly, the branch supporting his weight snapped and fell flat to the ground. The yelling wolf crashed onto it quickly after. Wulfur jumped back to avoid being hit by the debris.

"There. You see? You look stupid. Practice your climbing antics when we're not hiding from danger. Now, listen..."

The runt got up awkwardly and shook his fur pelt. He let his eyes wander, trying not to focus on his father. He cowered and started to fiddle with the torn leaves as Wulfur began to talk about the camp.

"In the past, I've used you as a means of distraction. This time, I will distract the humans whilst you go for the food."

"Really?" the runt squeaked as he sat down facing Wulfur.

"Really. I'm counting on you to be as swift as you can," Wulfur replied, also taking a rest on the grass. "The place is called... naterall resork eztrat... un... something. They got some-"

Wulfur's son put up both his paws in front of him and crossed them to interrupt.

"Hold up! How'd you know what it's called? You spoke to them?" he asked.

"I read the signpost," Wulfur replied, his glare turning ominous.

"You can read?" the runt questioned, his head raising slightly with his attention now diverted from the leaves underneath him.

Wulfur nodded. "Yes."

"Human words?"

"Yes, runt."

"How though?" The runts' expression turned cranky, as if he wanted Wulfur to pick up on his sarcasm. "Heh, is it another of those gifts from Ulfur, wolf god of might? Hahaha..."

The adolescent male's chuckle faded away as he saw the serious look on Wulfur's face. The golden wolf's joy rapidly declined.

"Heh... huh- urgh. Okay so you read it," he said, rolling his eyes. "What does it mean?"

"I'm not that sure," answered Wulfur, his eyes looking down at the grass. "But it looks like they are removing trees from our forests."

His son stamped a foot into the ground and snarled.

"Those inferior sub-gods. Can we stop it?"

Wulfur looked up at the runts' sudden determination. This had to be fake. He had never shown such confidence in his plans. He grunted, letting the young pup express the way he wanted to.

"Maybe. I want to find a way to sabotage whatever they use to start the fires. So, whilst you take the food, I will be destroying their tools..."

Wulfur then hesitated at the thought of the semi-large grey noise machine attached to the cabin. "...and I'm going to break their power box so that we can escape whilst they try to fix it."

"What are we waiting for?" the runt said, getting off his bottom and turning toward where Wulfur had come from. "Let's get 'em!"

Wulfur quickly got up and bit hard into his son's tail, stopping his advancement.

"No! Not yet!" he said through bared fangs. He let go of his tail and the runt wagged it between his legs. "Wait for nighttime. We'll be harder to spot."

They waited in silence for a moment as Wulfur preserved energy where he stood. He began to revise the layout of the camp in his head, assessing best entry points and escape routes. Even a thought on which structures would have the most meat inside.

The runt sat down again, realising he had been silly. Wulfur looked over at him, seeing humiliation bleed from his face. Noticing the tree responsible for delivering such humility to his son, Wulfur offered a lighter conversation as they both waited for the sun to set.

"That tree has a very high first branch. The trunk's thin too. I still don't know how you managed to climb it," Wulfur remarked.

There was a momentary pause as the air became cooler with the shadows of trees creeping up on them. The darkening sky graced them with the presence of the moon, still in the early stages of its' cycle. Wulfur looked up, admiring the twinkles of light appearing in the night sky. The runt joined in feeling obligated to copy his fathers' actions.

"I guess that deer gave me a lot of energy," the runt replied.

"Yes, but conserve now," Wulfur said, looking toward the young male, who appeared to be letting the sky's light pass right through him. "You'll need it."

Chapter 4

The night sky was clear. Constellations of stars could be seen from the seating areas of the camp. Many of the men on site were chatting about stories and sharing drinks whilst another guarded the marked entrance from the South. Wulfur and his son emerged from the East side, through the same needlegrass cover that he had scouted from. This was a good opportunity for him to show his boy the sight of the camp, so that he had a visual sense of the task at hand. The contained fire had been extinguished, but the area was still lit by some strange square light sources on thin stilts. There was a glow emitting through the gaps of the cabin too. Wulfur could hear a strange melodic sound. *'The humans sang songs too?'* he thought. He looked over at the runt with a confident show of teeth. He used his nose to point out what he was explaining.

"There, on the right, between the big building and the yellow boxes. I will knock something over to get their attention. Whilst I get into position, you're going to wait behind that far tent. When you hear the crash and the humans are distracted, get inside and take what you can. Be careful not to bump into a human on your way through."

The young wolf nodded after each point of interest was shown to him.

"When you've got as much food as you can carry, you can come back on yourself and return here. I should spot you. Or sneak to that stone thing on the far West. That's where I'll be."

Wulfur readied himself to jump down to the right when he saw his son looking anxious.

"Uh, father? What if I get caught?"

"Then sprint," Wulfur simply put. "They're powerless to catch you without their weapons. Escape before they can arm themselves."

Wulfur waited for his son to react. The golden wolf bowed his head, then Wulfur doing the same in response.

"Let's go," Wulfur whispered.

With that, the pair divided, a flash of gold diving down to the left and the timber beast slithering right, bound for the cabin.

The runt stayed on the green stuff until he was the shortest distance possible from the fourth tent along. Further from him, he heard a couple of humans in conversation on the wooden benches. To his right, he could see the armed guard at the stripey gate. The young male felt his legs shaking and tail curling under as his position was in line of sight with the guard. As long as he kept low, the guard wouldn't see him in the darkness. He readied himself, listening out for a sound to signal his next move. Hearing the crickets of the night, he swallowed and tensed up his shoulders. It wouldn't be long now.

On the East side, Wulfur padded up to an arrangement of red barrels. They appeared to have pictures of fire on their surfaces. This put his hackles up as he might have just poked his nose right onto a source of sub-god power. In a way, it invited him. He gave the barrel a lick, getting a tongue full of steel. He didn't react much to it but considered it a blessing to be this close. He quickly lowered his ears as he heard a human come within metres and reach into one of the sandy yellow supply crates. They pulled out a duck carcass. This is what he was after!

When the human moved away, Wulfur got up on his hind legs and snuffed his head into the box. He swiftly pulled out a couple of mallards by their heads and dragged them behind the crate. The smell of fresh meat filled his nose, and his hunting instinct was primed. Peering over the red barrels, he saw a human hold a tiny stick and strike it against a paw-sized box. The stick was lit with the fire of man. Wulfur watched as the human cast it into the pile of strewn wood and caused it to fire up once more.

Wulfur then noticed a larger box behind them filled to the top with metal utensils. Eager to initiate the signal, he crept around the barrels and threw both his paws at the box. It fell against another sealed crate and smashed on the gritted ground. Pots, pans and kitchen utensils sprung out and clanged into each other. Wulfur quickly whipped around and darted for the back of the crates on the far North.

The humans on this side of the camp quickly responded, walking directly toward the mess of equipment. Wulfur crept in the shadows with the prey until he was closer to the fire. On the bench, he saw the tiny device the human lit the fire with. Wulfur dropped the birds and confiscated it with his teeth. He left one of the birds behind to make room in his mouth and hoped that his son would make up for the rest of the take. Carrying the less fortunate mallard and a box that could start fires, Wulfur made a stealthy navigation around the hut and toward the well where he'd wait for the runt.

The sound of clanging metal was barely heard by the young wolf, but he took the guards' turn of head as the signal to go. He kept his paws light as he wiggled through the hedgerows until he was right behind the first tent.

He peered around the corner, watching a few humans walk up toward the circle of fire. Their chatter was untranslatable, and the scent of humans was overwhelming. The feeling of this hideout was also bizarre. Without wasting more time, he picked a moment and darted into the tent entrance. He shook on his way in, feeling agitated by the fabric that graced his fur.

It was dark inside, but a smell drew his attention to a metal locker. He needed to act fast, unaware of how long the humans were distracted for. He fiddled with the lock, but it would be futile, leaving only scratch marks on the door. The young male got both paws onto the handle and slipped on it. He backed off and grunted in frustration.

Suddenly the room lit up all around him and he heard a light gasp from behind. He turned his head and saw a human child from their bed staring right at him, holding a lit fire contained in a glass pod. The runt froze. He had been seen. He recalled being told to run, but he was too overwhelmed to think of it right away. His breathing had become rapid as he backed up into the corner closest to the exit.

What was this young human going to do? Would he cry "wolf"? He stared into the eyes of the child, hiding his ears, tail and teeth from view. He truly believed that he was going to die here. The little human looked at the scratches on the locker. Then, much to the runts' surprise, the child slowly got out of his bed, went up to the locker and grabbed something atop it. Then he put it inside the door, turned it and pulled it open.

The wolf watched, stunned like a still frame. The kid then stepped back from the open container and pointed at it with his limb. At first, the runt didn't understand what to think. The kid then made a grunt sound as he jolted a finger at the door once more.

The golden male slowly approached the container whilst maintaining eye contact with the child. His nose peered in, and he saw slabs of meat. After a brief sniff he recognised them as boar. Taking a mouthful, he quickly moved his head back from the cabinet, seeing the child quickly take cover in his bed again. Sat up he was, watching the runt back up to the exit. The human hadn't harmed him but instead had given him access to food. What was going on?

With no way to communicate with the child, the runt simply lowered his head as if to say thanks. Whether he should be trying to communicate with children of the sub-gods or not, was of the least importance right now. With the food in mouth, the wolf exited the tent with the child sat up, smiling, then blowing his light out.

As the golden wolf peered out the entrance, he once again felt the annoying friction of the flappy doors drifting over his fur. Barely able to process the feeling, he shivered in disgust and looked toward the commotion. There were plenty of humans still gathered there. His father must have made quite the mess.

Then a new smell caught the young wolf's attention. It was coming from the next hideout. Its door flaps were tied open this time. With eagerness, the runt followed his nose into the next tent without space in his jaw for any more food.

His nose followed the ground, leading him to a large bag. The top was open, and it contained an antler along with a few cooked salmon steaks and magpie feathers. The runt plunged his nose inside and accidentally dropped the boar meat amongst the rest. Panicking, he launched his jaw into the bag, gnashing on something rather soft. He pulled out a long, thick strap with bits of plastic bonding it to the mobile storage.

The runt stopped and then had a brainwave. He didn't need to carry the meat on its own. He could just carry it by this soft strap and all the food inside the bag would come along too. Realising this potential, he dropped the bag and looked around to see if he could make it a paws' worth. His father would be so proud of him.

The golden wolf then spotted another. This bag had a shiny rod sticking out of the open part and a few round badges sewn onto it. The runt quickly moved to it and began pulling at the strap with his teeth. It wasn't moving. He pulled harder, his rear paws pushing into the ground and tail stuck outward like a wizards' wand.

The bag then snapped away, pulling the cabinet over with it. The sudden release of tension threw the wolf back and he reared into a wooden rack, stocked with machetes. They then collapsed over the wolf, sinking sharp edges into his rump. The clunk of the cabinet and rack, along with the tiny sounds of painful yelping, alerted the humans from Wulfur's distraction, and they began to walk slowly toward the row of tents.

Wincing in pain, the golden wolf still clenched onto the straps as he tried to shake his body free from the wreckage. As he wriggled out, the sharp weapons impaled his skin and formed jagged edges across his hind from the weight of the rack. Eventually, he was out of the innovative deathtrap.

The potential for food in both carry things was too tempting to leave without. Hearing the footsteps of humans outside getting louder, the panicked wolf widened his jaw to grip both bags and limped out of the tent. He looked to his right and heard voices becoming louder. They were coming!

With his restricted movement, he cowered below a bench. He spotted a few humans now diverting their attention to the end of the path. His heart pounded, looking back at the second hideout he entered. His blood trail would surely be noticed.

The sound of whirring engines in the ambient air then stopped, and all the lights went out. The humans coming toward him stopped advancing and turned their heads in the direction of the cabin, which had a small support of light from the fire. *'What just happened?'* the golden wolf thought. The humans would have a harder time seeing him in the dark... that's what his father had said. Maybe he did something to eliminate the light?

He could not waste any more time. The runt made a dash from the bench cover and bolted it toward the stone where his father said he would be. He looked down and spotted a tiny box in the dirt alongside a bird carcass.

"Runt!"

The young male jumped and flicked his head around, seeing his father sprinting from the same place he had just been hiding.

"Father, I'm hurt!" the young wolf moaned, now feeling the cuts on his rear sting more from his frantic movements.

"Go, go, go! Up the hill. Quickly!" Wulfur instructed.

The runt felt a reassuring sense of relief, but he done as he was told and ran into the wilderness, bound for the vantage point some two-hundred metres away. Wulfur followed, picking up the last food scrap and the matchbox, catching up to his son in a matter of seconds. His eyes were wide with confusion at the bizarre items the boy was carrying. The smell of many food types filled his nose. He took a second look at his son's tail as blood flicked off from it. He concluded that he wouldn't stop now to ask why. Better they both got well out the way of danger first.

The camps' lights came back on, and the runt halted for a moment to see, letting his father dash past him. He panted vigorously, trying to make out what the humans were doing through his blurred eyes.

The same child he encountered approached a taller human. Was he telling them about seeing a wolf in the tent? He watched their upper limbs flail around until he caught the female giving a warm hug to the child. They must have been worried for him. The golden male felt wind in his fur as he thought for a moment about how his own father embraced him. It wasn't possible that these humans had feelings too, right? They are the sub-gods of the land after all and only want to destroy the wolves. Why did the boy spare him *and* willingly offer food? Thoughts kept inside, he got moving again, trailing his father by a long way.

Wulfur made it to the highest timber stump on the hill and lay flat on the floor, absorbing all the sights of the human camp in his head. He felt for sure that too much exposure might have driven him to insanity. He had done it. He infiltrated a human camp. It would be a tale so extraordinary that future generations wouldn't be able to comprehend his bravery enough.

Finally, the runt made it to the top as well, seeing his father laying like roadkill. He dropped the pair of bags with a loud thud, making Wulfur's ears rotate behind him. Wulfur kept his eyes closed as his adrenaline-fuelled smile disappeared.

"What have you got there?" he asked the runt.

"Look at the size of these, father! Ow!"

The runt winced, looking back at his tail and seeing much of his fur stained red. He tried to sit down, but his leg muscles were sore from the knife cuts and would ooze more pain when he tried to contract them into his hips. He wiggled his legs until he was standing up straight again, then tried to fall on his side, using his front paws as support. He slouched over whilst looking at his father.

Wulfur turned to see the large duffle bags.

"We can't eat those," his father muttered. "What else is there?"

"But look, inside," exclaimed his son, pointing at the top with his nose.

Wulfur got up, still looking strong and athletic. He went up to the lighter bag, seeing its open top and took a sniff. There was plenty of meat here. Boar, salmon... an antler? *'Could be good to relieve toothache,'* he thought. Some magpie feathers... this was impressive. He had doubted the young male would have brought out more food than him let alone triple. But there was another bag. He couldn't wait to see inside it.

"This is really good, son."

The runt was too busy licking the blood off his tail to respond to his fathers' compliment. Wulfur approached the second bag. But he slowed before reaching the zipper and saw the long thin metal barrel sticking out of it. He then slowly turned his head toward his son in dubiousness.

"What... did you...?" The timber male was lost for words as he clenched his fangs around the zip and pulled carefully. He let go and gawped at the sight. The runt paused with his tongue out, now observing his fathers' reaction.

"You stole a... black magic contraption?" he whispered, looking over at the runt, eyes full of disbelief.

"I did?" The runt was confused. "I just saw the shiny stick and I... couldn't resist it."

Wulfur sat up on his hind and placed a paw on the mystic item. The touch was cold and lifeless. The sudden sense of death crept up Wulfur's leg like a squirrel up a tree. He shivered, then pushed it away very quickly, unsure if it would do anything to him.

The runt finished tending to his injuries and watched in silence with his head tilted slightly. Wulfur then got both paws around the metal barrel and wiggled it free of the bag. Then he tossed it away from him into the open. It hit the ground with a thud and Wulfur looked somewhat stunned.

'This looks like something the humans used to fight the ancestors,' he thought speculatively. He dared not meddle with its' power. He didn't know how it worked and that's what unsettled him. Now the runt could have a good look at it. The object appeared to be a metallic tube wedged into a thicker base of wood, with a few smaller shinier pieces underneath.

For Wulfur, he felt dizzy. He wanted to see what else his son had made off with. At least that would take his mind off the black magic for a moment. He buried his nose into the bag, feeling some other hard items. He clasped his jaws around a very small, bone-like shard and spat it out on the floor. It looked like... a wolf tooth. Wulfur quickly put a paw in his mouth to check if it were his.

"Runt, did you lose any teeth whilst you were in the-" his voice juddered to a halt when he turned to see his son holding the wooden stock against his flank and attempting to chew at the top of the barrel. The weapon made light clicking noises around where the young wolf was suspending it between his paws. Wulfur was shocked at the sight of the runt playing with the weapon like it were a toy. "Runt! Stop! That thing is pointing at you!"

The golden male looked over to see how serious his father was. The timber wolf had stood up with his front legs poised apart and his tail flailing between his legs. The runt reluctantly let go of the barrel from his grip and begun to lick its' side.

"But the metal bit is so pretty."

Wulfur didn't believe what he was hearing. *'This wolf had mush for brains,'* he thought. That contraption had a way to be activated, and he wasn't going to allow his son to line himself up for death. He turned his head away to resume his interest in the bag, concluding that the tooth had been acquired by a human hunter. *'Some unlucky wolf likely got their fang kept as a trophy. Well, fangs,'* he imagined, seeing yet another wolf tooth underneath a pronghorn antler. *'Whoever this bag belonged to... they were quite the collector.'*

He noiselessly chuckled as he knew it belonged to him now. He pushed over a strange transparent water container to pick up a golden item in his jaws. It was round with a loose bit of metal dangling on one side and made Wulfur's ears twitch. It was making a sound. It mimicked the sound of crickets from very far away. Less of a chirp, but more of a click. And it clicked at the same rate... all the time.

"Here, runt. You like shiny things? Check this out," he mumbled through his full mouth. Wulfur swung his head so that the gold ticker was hurled out of his jaw toward the runt. He had laid the weapon on the ground, still licking away at its silver barrel. His eyes beamed up, seeing the even shinier roller come to him. He stumbled as he got to his feet and caught his hind paw under the wooden stock to come up and see it. He took a sniff and then absorbed that ambient ticking noise. The young male was fascinated.

"Oh, more gold," his father announced sarcastically, now throwing the objects at the runts' face.

The golden male felt the small gold fragments bop him on the snout. These items were round as well but very tiny. They appeared to have an inscription on each of them. The image of a human head.

"These are amazing!" complimented the runt. "Ow! Careful, that nearly hit my eye."

Wulfur ignored him. "Mhmm, yeah. There's no food in this, runt. A waste of your energy. You only needed to steal food. Not this heavy sack of junk."

"I didn't have time to see what was inside, father," his son argued. "They were coming. I think I did right to just take it and go. Besides, we got an extra err... thing to put food into."

"Ah no, no, no, no... you can't be serious," Wulfur exclaimed. "We are not taking both of these... *ginormous* food holders with us. A talon will be fine."

"But look at how much food we can keep," the runt pointed out. "You wanted that 'head start' with making wolves believe you're powerful. Well, this is perfect. Don't you see?"

"Runt, we need to be agile." Wulfur's voice began to intensify. "We'll be easy targets for food. And don't you dare try to tutor me about the benefits of something we took from the humans! You're pathetic!"

In rage, Wulfur slung the emptied bag with all his upper body strength up the tree behind him. The bag somersaulted over one of its' branches and then fell directly over Wulfur's head, leaving him sightless as he turned back to the runt. He looked daft. The runt tried his best to hold his cool, but a small snort still managed to escape.

"Rargh! It's not funny!" Wulfur yelled from inside the bag. He scrambled his paws over the top to try and get it off. When it slid off his face, he gripped his claws in very hard, wanting to curse at the bag. Then he stopped. Before his eyes, he saw the row of badges sewn to its exterior. The left and middle badges had pictures of mountains and trees, whilst the third had a pair of simple black lines crossing each other through the middle. It also had some human writing sewn above the 'X'.

Wulfur read it, then lowered the bag to look at his ear-sloped son. Then raised the bag again. His ears began to twitch slightly, the lines and shapes spoke clear words to him like another wolf whispering in his ear. He let out a light gasp whilst hearing in his head, a tone reminiscent of an elder wolf, what the symbols meant.

"I'll carry both carry things if it bothers you that much," his son mumbled. "It looks like part of them can be hung around my shoulders."

"Elite... How does that sound?" Wulfur asked.

"I'm sorry, what?" the golden wolf replied, leaning his head forward.

Wulfur chucked the bag at him, the runt with an outstanding catch in both paws.

"Look on the back," Wulfur instructed. "The inscription says Elite. And since it's the holder you were most curious about, that can be your name."

The runt looked at the badge. He couldn't read it. Instead, he just repeated it in his head as he observed the symbols.

"Elite... that's not so bad. I like it. What does it mean?"

"I don't know," Wulfur admitted. "But no wolf will know its meaning either. That's what's going to set you apart from the others. You're named something special. Now let's move. Ditch the junk and let's go."

He got up to leave and grabbed the bag of fresh food with his fangs. His nose indulged in the essence of meats and meditated at the thought of full bellies. The runt watched as his father walked toward the rear side of the hill, away from the camp. For a moment, he beamed, hearing that he had finally earned a name. After a nest of moons wandering this land of mortality, his father had given him an identity that wasn't downgrading or offensive.

A light giggle escaped the young wolf's maw as he looked down at all the stuff they had stolen and then saw inside the bag. It wasn't completely empty. At the bottom was a paper-thin square. He observed closely and saw that it contained a realistic image of three humans looking at him. His eyes widened with intrigue.

"No, actually father, I'm taking it with us," the young male declared with a smile like a youngster had on their birthday. He was joyously contemplating his new name in his head. Elite. The name meant 'him'. And his father approved of it. He hadn't known his father to agree to much in his favour.

Wulfur's brows furrowed above his closed eyes. "Don't be silly, we don't need both," he said, once again his voice muffled from holding the strap between his teeth.

"But these flappy bits," the young male argued. "I think I see a way to keep both without slowing us down."

"You're being delusional. Forget it... Elite." Wulfur stopped for a moment, then chuckled slightly. He turned his head and viewed his son from over his shoulder, seeing him scramble to pick up the inedible objects in his paws and teeth. "I like the name too. Alright, you can keep it for now. Just promise me you'll ditch it to save your life."

The runt nudged his head inside the space between the bag and its' strap to test if his theory worked. As he felt it slide behind his neck, he got up and felt the weight of the load suspend on his right side. It worked for now, but it would need adjusting. He moved toward his father, leaving behind a patch of blood from his rump injury.

"Yes, father," Elite said happily. "By next moon, you'll be wishing you never doubted me!"

"Whatever," the timber male responded, taking a formal trod down toward a huge landscape of green, illuminated by the moon. He inhaled deeply through his nostrils reflecting on his power of reading the human language, hoping that it was indeed the Greater One, Ulfur, who had spoken to him. But in trust of how the scenery ahead looked, he hoped for a long break from seeing the humans again, or anything to do with them. His son, now named Elite, followed behind with a smug grin and a few light wounds on his tail.

The moon was descending, but for as long as it was up, the sound of many wolves could be heard howling at it. Wulfur took in the sound, realising how much closer they were. He thought it wouldn't be far to go before they'd find another den to disrupt. Wulfur with a desire to shake up the natural order of the forest, and his son Elite, who may not have an end goal beyond helping his father, now had a name to be remembered by.

Wulfur and Elite journey through the many acres of unclaimed land, searching for their kind. A paw of moons would pass with their objective still the same: infiltrate dens and steal food.
In this time, Wulfur would bear witness to his son successfully climbing a tree, as a result, realising its' potential. Up in the tree, Elite would see the Wise Wolfs' hideout to their North. Wulfur confidently decides to head the other way. Elite needed to be toughened up first before attempting to take him down.
Carrying the weight of both bags on his shoulders, Elite had shown off his balance capabilities to Wulfur on a fallen tree log. He accidentally slips and falls, a sharp branch impaling his belly on landing. Despite the foolish move, Wulfur didn't hesitate to aid Elite, fetching leaves to press against the wound. As Elite healed up, Wulfur collected specific herbs around the forest. They would be useful for something later.
The pair would get moving once the bleeding had stopped. Wulfur gave time to Elite, helping him practice combat. Even teaching him how to assert dominance. Unbeknownst to them, a crow glided above the trees. It watched their every move, Elite in particular.

Back at the waterfall, the Wise Wolf quietly watched the forest toward the East with a freshly picked heather between his paws. He saw the form of another wolf take shape out of the forage. She had a pelt of silver and white, her eyes holding a tamed fire within her soul. She approached the Wise Wolf and peered at the heather. They would nuzzle heads before discussing certain news.

At the human camp, the hunter who had shot at Wulfur was looking around the tents. Something was missing. The young child who had witnessed Elite's antics held up a crumbled piece of paper to the hunter. On it was a scribble of a wolf he had done using yellow crayons. The hunter smiled and put his hand on the child's shoulder before turning his attention to a map. He pointed to a place further North, past the broken woods and the waterfall.

Chapter 5

A pair of wolves trekked along a worn pathway that boasted a wall of thick berry bushes. The taller, mature male took a sniff of the spring air and closed his eyes, feeling the wave of heat absorb into his eyelids and the gentle warm breeze glistening against his light brown coat. The other wolf alongside him was a young female with a mixture of browns and reds except for the chest and snout, which had a dabble of creamy white. The midday sun lit up her pelt, speckling her back with a stroke of orange. The moisture on her nose was so rich, it dripped off her face as she spoke. Her voice was sour but energetic.

"So, if the hare makes it to the burrow before I catch it, I go wait at a different hole?" she asked the taller wolf.

"That's right, Jeeva," he replied. "It's better to guess the next hole he'll emerge from as he remembers that he last saw you where he shoved his ugly pom-tail into."

"That's really good advice, mentor Quade."

They both stopped and the mentor wolf gave her a friendly, inviting smile.

"Please, just call me Quade. It really is a lot of fun teaching you to hunt. I'm sure the Alpha would be very pleased with your skills."

Jeeva smiled back. She was rather fond of her mentor. She let her mind wander for a second, then she lowered her head and swooped her ears behind.

"What about my brother?"

Quade tried to resist reacting to who she spoke of. But he let out an angry sigh.

"Oh, that coyote brain? He is nothing compared to you. I can't even get him to-" Then a loud sequence of yapping came from across the clearing. "Uhhh, speaking of that..."

Out from a thicket of rosemary bushes jumped an excitable timber-pelted young male. He bounced around left and right like a wobbly thimble.

"Ooh, hoo! Mentor Quade!" he shouted in joy. "Hah-hah! Where are we scouting today? Huh? Where? Is it just over here?"

"Arvy, I'm training Jeeva today."

"Oh, yeah! Ha! Hi, sis!"

The looney wolf stuck his tongue out to the side and play-bowed in front of Jeeva. Quade crunched his face and let out a faint growl. Jeeva kept her head down, trying to lose Arvy's attention.

"Hey, have you noticed how little clouds there are in the sky today?" the crazed wolf asked. "Hee-hee... Maybe they migrated just like the birds!"

Jeeva tried to speak for her mentor, so he didn't have to get aggressive. "Clouds don't migrate, Arvux. And it's spring. The birds have all come back."

"Oh yeah! Silly me!" Arvux tilted his head, allowing his tongue to get off the ground. He danced his way across the path, holding his play-bow form. Quade had had enough.

"If you're looking for an assignment, I'll give you it," he said, stepping forward.

Arvux sprung in delight. "Ooh, yeah! Please! I'll do anything for you! And for me!"

Quade then waved his left paw at the red berry bush.

"See those berries? The only way to scout them properly is to eat them."

Arvux ceased his dance and tilted his head. His body was loose and relaxed.

"Why?" he asked.

"Because um... er... you can... work out bird migration patterns based on their taste," Quade replied, his eyes wandering into the sky whilst he sighed heavily between breaths.

Arvux then observed the berries with his head still on a tilt. Then his tongue slid back inside his mouth.

"Sounds good to me! I'll do it!"

Jeeva looked up to witness Arvux's acceptance of Quade's theory. She took in some air through her front teeth and flurried her ears. She then shook her pelt and sat down to watch this assignment unfold. This was clearly a trick her mentor was setting him up for.

Arvux bolted toward the berry bush and stopped to see the range before him.

"Ooh do I eat this? Or this! No, the other was better... no, wait! This, um..." he danced around the shrubberies observing the different formations of tempting fruit.

"Just pick that berry you're looking at!" Quade called out.

"Huh, okay!" he shouted in excitement and took a mouthful of the red stuff without hesitation. In his own world, he crunched the fruit, causing the juice to explode and stain his gums. He giggled a little at first, feeling great about what he was doing. But then, his excitement dissolved as he grunted and opened his jaw to let the contents slide out. He spat and snorted at the ground, strings of saliva still connecting from his tongue to the earth.

Quade sat proudly from a few metres back, watching his prank succeed. He scoffed with a narcissistic grin and looked over to Jeeva.

"You see?" he commented quietly. Jeeva looked up at her mentor. "Your brother's a moron. He'll be an omega soon enough. C'mon, laugh with me."

"I just don't understand why it's so hard for him to learn," Jeeva whispered. She kept her head low and didn't let her body hiccup from Quade's sense of humour. "I know our mother accidentally squashed him as a pup during sleep, but I didn't know it was going to make him the way he is today."

"Don't focus on his future, focus on yours," her mentor replied.

Arvux was still spitting and kept a look of enthusiasm across his face.

"Look! I did it! I guess the birds are going South!"

Quade spoke with a tone of unassured praise.

"Yes, well done Arvy. Now follow behind quietly. And I mean quietly! Me and Jeeva have much to discuss." He and Jeeva got up at the same time and began to advance down the path. Arvux stood still and watched them head East.

"Oh, sure! Hahaha," he said, then gasped. "Are we heading back?"

"Yes, Arvy. Remember? Back around the mound of forest. You can't shortcut through here. We then head back on ourselves, and we'll be in the open fields. Pack entrance will be in sight by then."

"I know that, haha. We're so close from this side, I can almost taste it!" Arvux replied, exposing his tongue again.

As Quade walked with Jeeva by his side, he looked over his shoulder at Arvux, his eyes blazing with vexation.

"I'm telling you it again, because you exhausted our search party. Now shut your mouth and stay close!"

Arvux calmed behind Quade, hearing him raise his voice in frustration.

"Oh, right! Of course. Quiet. Yeah. I'll be that."

Jeeva avoided joining in, choosing to listen to Quade neutralise her brother from being a bother. She looked ahead and diverted her attention to smells in the air. Her powerful hunting nose picked up on something unfamiliar.

"Um, Quade," she muttered. "There's an odd smell coming up ahead."

The mentor wolf raised his nose and sniffed around. "I'm not catching anything, dear Jeeva."

Arvux, now chasing a butterfly, darted around behind them to keep up with it. The little insect flapped its blue wings calmly and then flew out the way of Arvux's view. That was then when Arvux froze, his eyes widened.

"Ha-ooh! Stranger danger! Hide! Hide!" he bellowed, charging for the nearest gap in the forage to his left.

Quade watched him and tutted. "Arvy, I said shut your-" he stopped to look ahead. There were a couple of wolves coming their way. They didn't look familiar. "Yikes, Jeeva. Quick! Into the brush with Arvy."

Without saying anything, Jeeva nodded and jumped over the plants, trying to avoid getting chlorophyll in her fur. Then Quade trotted on into the darkness after her.

The approaching wolves were Wulfur and Elite. They both still had the duffel bags from the human camp. Wulfur had the lighter bag, the stench of prey oozing out of the top where the zipper hadn't fully been closed. Elite's bag weighed more, containing the weapon, some extra items Wulfur wanted for the future, and all the other beautiful trinkets Elite had wanted to keep.

"What did you say those herbs were for?" Elite asked his father, his focus taking a quick detour to the bag on his shoulder.

"You forgot already?" Wulfur said, rolling his eyes. "We burn them and then put out the fire with some water. I've seen the effects. I've... experienced the effects."

"Don't talk bogus," Elite taunted, his tone more confident than it had been the moon before. "It's just a hot pot of lavender with some spicy slop. It's completely unnecessary."

"You might be a bigger and smarter wolf now..." Wulfur continued, giving his son a fiery glare. "But you're still continuously arrogant. I cannot fix that."

"But why do you care how I behave?" Elite said as his eyebrows tried to drop further than they physically could. "We've spent so long trying to find another place. You said we were close all the way back at the human camp, and we've now been on the move for weeks. Stop lying to me, I'm getting sick of it!" His voice turned snappy. He had a small show of fangs lined up at his father.

"Hold up, Elite..." Wulfur interrupted. "I smell trouble. Keep your senses alert."

Elite glared at his father and hid his teeth. He sniffed the air aggressively, making his frustrations clear. His nasal cartilage then untensed, allowing him to try and pick up whatever scent his father had noticed.

The duo reached the point on the path where Quade and his group had hidden across on their right. The three of them watched through the tall grass as they passed and begun to whisper.

"Is that... the pair of wolves the messenger spoke of?" Jeeva asked. "A talon timber and the other gold."

"Not likely," replied Quade. "We got that warning moons ago." He looked again at the bizarre attire on the golden wolf's back. "Well, we *could* find out if they're dangerous."

"How?" Jeeva asked him.

Grinning, Quade looked over at Arvux who had caught the butterfly in his mouth. He only spat it out to return an eager glance at Quade.

Wulfur leant his head down to sniff the trail. "Multiple wolves. Hopefully a den is nearby." Elite didn't respond. He just rolled his eyes and kept trudging along.

Suddenly, a gasp came from the bushes, then Arvux flew out of the hiding spot, landing face first onto the path. His hind legs were dangling in the air and his tail hung over his head. Hearing the commotion, both Wulfur and Elite turned to see who was there. Wulfur stared with surprise and Elite had to look twice to make sure he wasn't imagining things.

"Hi!" Arvux said playfully. He let his tongue poke out. His eyes were crossed inward, and his tail wagged softly.

Wulfur turned to face the looney wolf and spoke first. His tone was vigorous.

"Who are you?"

Arvux excitedly fell on his belly and got to his feet as quickly as he could. What a great question! The curiosity he imagined the muscular stranger to have peaked his excitement. He playfully bounced around, not taking any regard for the chance of hostility.

"Wap! Bap! Woohoo! Me? I have a lot of names," he proudly shouted, his paws flailing in the air like a flightless bird. "Arvux, Arvy, Arvus, Arvo, Fickle, Coyotebrain, Gigglesnort. Hey! Did you want to add something new?"

Wulfur held still as the crazy wolf danced in front of him. Arvux got onto his hind paws like a stallion. The energy in this wolf was ridiculous. So long as Arvux didn't touch him, Wulfur had no reason to defend himself. He also considered that a wolf this high on ancestral moondust wouldn't be a loner. Wulfur imagined him dead within a few suns.

"Ah, no," Wulfur replied followed up by an uninspired sigh. "Are you from any sort of ...aspect?"

From the bushes, the other wolves kept quiet. Hearing this question, Jeeva looked toward Quade and whispered lighter than the rustle of leaves. "Quade, we need to stop him. He's going to tell them everything."

"Shh..." Quade filled in. "They don't look that interested. Especially the yellow wolf. He looks like he wants to run away whilst the big brute's not looking."

Arvux then approached Elite, making a nosedive for his bag. "Ooh, what is that?"

Elite snarled and raised the hackles on his back that weren't buried by the bag supports.

"Back off!" he snapped.

"Oh, sorry!" Arvux yelled in excitement.

"Hey! I asked you a question!" Wulfur shouted at him. "Where'd you come from?"

Arvux whipped around, seeing the massive fangs on the old timber wolf. He fidgeted and frisked back toward where Wulfur stood.

"Oh yeah, my bad, so you can call me Arvy. I'm from the pack of unquiet dreams. We're quite the happy bunch, haha."

Elite tilted his head and allowed his fangs to hide away under his lips. "Pack of unqui... what?!" His paws began to clench.

Wulfur sighed and turned to Elite, "Well, there certainly isn't anything quiet about *this* wolf."

"Urgh, I already don't like him," Elite remarked. "Can we just go? Keep your senses alert my crupper!"

Stamping his foot into the ground, Elite turned and began to walk by himself along the path they were headed before. Wulfur turned to leave as well, taking his son's reaction into account. But then Arvux spoke again.

"And if you ever wanted to visit, you could follow back this way and take a right onto the open fields, and we are at the other end!"

It spiked Wulfur's curiosity that this gathering of wolves was also referred to as a "pack". *'Great,'* he thought. *'Another bunch of Greater Ones backbiters.'* This was no longer a hindsight. It was a rising issue. Wulfur knew deep down the ways of the ancestors but hadn't told Elite much at all.

There appeared to be some manipulation going on in the surrounding land. Believing in The Greater Ones was normal but there was never anything to justify the need of pack hierarchy. Wulfur stopped and turned his head to Arvux. If this information was true, he'd be on to another great plan.

"What count are in this pack?" Wulfur asked, his stare now locked onto Arvux.

"What? Wolves?" Arvux replied, looking at his paws to assist with counting. "Erm... a nest, a paw and a paw."

'Not that many then,' Wulfur thought. This pack didn't sound like anything as militant as the Astral Order, an aspect he'd only heard stories of. "And hunters?" Wulfur clenched his claws into the dirt and raised the hackles in his spine.

"Um, a paw, no! A talon and paw!" Arvux corrected excitedly.

"And what about food?" Wulfur followed with, his tone deepening with his growth of knowledge. "Do you have a stash?"

The crazy wolf pinned his own paws close together and leaned up close to Wulfur's face.

"Of course we do! It's got some hare, goat, weasel! Ooh! Even *I* was on it once. But it was part of a prank to get me in trouble with the Alpha, hahaha!"

From the bushes, Jeeva was trying to signal Arvux to stop talking. She made small waves of her paws and shook her head violently. But she was too afraid to reveal herself or disappoint her mentor. Quade, however, kept cool and collected.

"Stop worrying, Jeeva. They're not going to come after us," he whispered, patting her neck with his paw. "We'll get you some water from Naito's hideout. That'll make you feel better."

Jeeva smoothly pirouetted her head toward Quade and gave him a frown when she heard that name.

"Yes... Naito..." she replied as quietly as breath. She shrugged tensely. "Bit of an oddball himself too."

Wulfur looked up the hill as Arvux spoke of the food and could see that Elite had stopped at the top of the slope, waiting for him.

"Okay I've heard enough," he declared. "Begone with you."

"Actually, you can meet my friends right now! They're-" Before Arvux could reveal his nearby packmates, Wulfur rammed his head into Arvux's belly whilst his head was turned to the bushes. He forcefully knocked him into a muddy patch that laid against the thick forest. Arvux grunted as his landing filled his nostrils with mud and worms.

Wulfur stood still for a moment and cackled at the fallen freak. He then set off after Elite. To make sure that the looney wolf didn't immediately follow him, he ran up the hill, kicking dirt behind him to fill the air with a brown haze.

Arvux coughed and choked, getting up to see Quade and Jeeva inside the bush cover. Jeeva was shaking her head with a stern look on her face. Quade peered up the hill to see if the pair of stranger wolves had vanished. Once they were out of sight, he emerged to see the capsized wolf.

"You need to work on not being such a loose mouth," scolded Quade. "I doubt they were the wolves that we were warned about but…"

"Yes, they were!" Jeeva interrupted.

Quade raised a paw formally at Jeeva's side.

"Not now, Jeeva. As for you Arvux, at least they didn't kill you."

Arvux lifted his head from the mud to look at his mentor in the eyes.

"Did I do good, mentor Quade?"

Quade did not answer that question and instead began walking down the path toward home, turning blind eye to Arvux. He spoke more loudly this time after checking behind him that the stranger wolves hadn't changed their minds.

"Worry not, both of you. I doubt they'll ever come back."

As Arvux got up, Jeeva approached, not looking as sympathetic as she did before the encounter.

"Mentor Quade is right. You really *are* a moron."

Arvux let his tongue loose again and then rapidly shook his fur coat, sending dirt particles into the air. Some of them landed on Jeeva's fur.

"No wait- arrgh!" She growled at Arvux.

The looney wolf laughed nervously as Jeeva approached. She pushed both her paws into Arvux's side, knocking him into the mud a second time. Backing off fast to avoid another dirt splash, Jeeva let out a small grin.

"Ooh, that felt good," she told herself. Then began following Quade's footsteps. But not so fast that Arvux would lose them.

They'd be home soon with some fresh water to drink... and get clean in. She stopped in her tracks again just before taking a right at the tree toward the field. She could see Arvux taking a slow walk behind, but she set her sights in the distance, now worried about those mysterious stranger wolves. The wolves she was sure they had been warned of.

Returning her attention to Arvux, she started to be encouraging to him. She was his sister after all, she felt it was important to keep his hopes up.

"C'mon Arvy! Let's go home. I would hate to see you get eaten by worms looking like that."

Hearing his sister cry out playfully, the smile on his face gleamed again as he started to catch up, bouncing all the way.

"Yeah, yeah!" Arvux responded in joy. The thought of food and shelter took over his mindset, blurring his vision of the encounter he just had. Around the tree they went, out into the open fields, on course for home.

"Say..." Arvux turned to Jeeva. "...who were those wolves?"

Chapter 6

The gently sloped path that took Wulfur and Elite further West reached its peak in altitude. Elite observed the many miles of forest ahead and could see a range of hills in a fog of tundra. He looked back at his father. Wulfur had only just caught up with him. Elite frowned but tried to keep himself from lowering his head.

The old wolf slowed up just before standing alongside him. He strained his front legs and grunted in infringement.

"Now hold on just a moment. Where do you think you're going?" he turned to Elite.

"Father, if we make it past those hills ahead, we could be somewhere completely new," the golden male replied.

Wulfur stomped his foot into the wavey buffalograss, flattening the unfortunate plants under his paw.

"That wolf back there said they have a prey pile," Wulfur detailed. "And only a paw and talon of hunters. That's a steal!" His face was filled with pure determination.

Elite's brows lowered even more, almost shielding his eyelids from the wind.

"Father, you can't be serious. Did you see that looney? I'm not going into a pack where the wolves are all out of their heads like that...that... jester of the shrubbery. Arvo... whatever his name was. Striking that pack is pointless."

He began to walk down the summit toward the thickening fog. Only three steps in and Elite felt a sting on his tail. He turned to see his father have a grip on him by the teeth. He spoke through his gritted fangs.

"Listen, I know pack law better than you, no matter how stupid the concept of a pack is. That lunatic was probably an omega."

He let go of his son's tail tip and retreated his head back up to its dominant rest spot. Elite relaxed and turned sideways at him, the sunlight illuminating gold out of his fluffy neck scruff. He had a stern look on his face.

Wulfur continued. "I reckon their den is strong. It explains why he's out here being a sly fox. They don't want him around. We should infiltrate them. I know we have spent moons in this forsaken forest, so this is our best opportunity." He took this pause of breath as an excuse to observe his surroundings. Elite was right. There was sight of a hilltop that could send them to a new part of the land. But why should he throw away this opportunity? There was also an area to their right, toward the North, of taller, thicker trees. Wulfur could smell a swamp. Easy ground prey perhaps.

In the moment of thought, Wulfur looked back at his son to find he had moved right up to his face and had outrage burning through his cheeks.

"No!" Elite bellowed. "I'm not going! You know what happened last time!" With a huff, Elite turned around and traversed up the narrow path.

"ELITE, DON'T YOU DARE WALK AWAY FROM-" Wulfur stopped himself from shouting at Elite. He closed his eyes and let out a low grumble. He turned his head slightly away from the linear view of his son before replying in a tone relatable to subdued thunder. "If I can't convince you then so be it. We are going this way," he instructed, pointing his snout toward where he could smell the swampy terrain.

Elite stopped, hearing word of his father going a different direction to him. It wasn't toward that pack, so he lifted his head up to listen some more.

"Let's hunt something together. Take your mind off that wolf from the upside-down," Wulfur suggested. "But understand me when I say we are not leaving the territory until we make an impact on that... pack." It kept paining Wulfur to say it. But he tried to retain the ounce of optimism he had left for this plan. "It's the only group we've learned of in moons. If you just learn from your mistakes all those times before, you'll be fine. Now let's get food." Wulfur turned toward the gap between trees which took them off the eroded pathway.

Reluctantly, Elite followed, knowing that he wouldn't know where to be without his father. But he felt more ambitious about those hills. For a little moment, the golden male lowered his head and thought about the possibilities of going that way. What he would see. What he'd encounter. How much confidence he would have to go at it alone.

He trailed his father into the darkness and observed the trees around him. They were built strong with sturdy branches. He thought about all the climbing he could practice too. He recalled doing similar things the moon before. At least if they were chased by a larger animal, they'd have a place to be safe... or so far that's what Elite thought would happen. He hadn't needed to climb a tree to save his life yet, so he had no idea how effective it would be.

For a while, the pair crept over the coarse dirt and rock to find little openings where burrows and tree roots dotted the landscape. Carrying on through, Wulfur had his ears and nose primed for hunting prey whilst making agile movements between the overgrown roots in their way.

Elite further back moved more slowly with his carry weight. He stopped suddenly under no intention of his own, feeling the bag pull against him. It was caught on a thick root curling up and out of the ground. The golden wolf gasped and reversed to try and loosen himself from it. When the root let go, he slid on his legs trying to restore his balance.

Wulfur stopped and turned to Elite, seeing his chest puff in and out rapidly. He slightly lowered his head with very little expression to show for.

"You're having a thought about that tree incident?" he asked.

"No?" Elite replied with a wobble in his speech.

"I'd imagine your belly must have healed up by now," said Wulfur, eyeing the area behind Elite's left shoulder. "How is it?"

Elite looked at his side, but didn't have a visual, since his gear was obscuring it. He wished he had never slipped off that collapsed tree trunk. He had felt rather foolish in the moment.

"It's fine," he declared.

Wulfur let out a sigh that came out as a grunt.

"Well, at least you're moving around a lot faster. Now what's say we get all that dens' food later, hm? Imagine how much of their stash we can get in them carry things…"

Wulfur imagined the many moons they'd have not going hungry. All they had to do was deplete any den's food stash and their food troubles would be at an end.

Wulfur felt himself let a delightful scoff escape, and that's when he stopped. He quickly realised he was starting to sound like his son. The level of enthusiasm for such petty things. Those bags. He hated to admit that Elite was right all along. It made him feel sick.

Thankfully, before he could barf, the smell of an animal whipped around his nostrils like a lasso. He took in a short breath before tensing up his body. Elite looked on with lack of interest, now taking a slow and cautious walk away from the root that struck his bag. It seemed like he got away without tearing it.

"Elite," his father quickly said. "Muskrat. Somewhere this way. Follow."

"Yes, father." Elite sounded like a bored pup in herbs class.

Feeling weary, the golden wolf followed his father into a crevasse of rock, leading to a clearing amongst the pale mist. The area had many holes in the ground. This could be where their scented prey was hiding.

Wulfur's voice became a whisper.

"Alright, Elite. They're going to be here. I'll coax them out by making a ruckus on this side. I need you to silently wait on the opposite side ready to strike. Got it?"

"Yeah, course I will," the young male replied, his voice held above a whisper as if he had no interest in playing his father's stealth game.

Wulfur nodded then shook his duffel bag off his neck before moving into the clear space to guard one of the holes. When he stopped, his eyes fixated on a symbol marked in the ground. A wolf had been here before. The marking was of a pair of paw pads with a pair of lines cutting through them. It was the symbol wolves used for sharing hunting grounds. Wulfur scowled at it before grinding his paw over the marking. When it was rendered non-existent, he resumed his stance, ready to scare prey. When he looked up, Elite had already got into position on the other side.

The golden male lowered his head to the ground, letting the straps slide over his scruff, scalp and snout. The bag quietly puffed a cloud of dirt, making Elite's golden fur pelt matted and dull in the gloomy atmosphere. The sound of dragonflies and frogs were the only things breaking the silence as they both readied up.

Elite looked at his father from across the clearing. Then at the hole beneath him. The dusty tunnel that leads to a supposed complex where muskrats liked to hide in. But then a glimmer caught Elite's eye. His head turned to an obscure colour poking out from the flat dirt. It was round on the top and boasted a unique texture on the surface. Seeing this, Elite took a step to his right, away from the hole he was meant to be fixated on.

Wulfur hadn't noticed the diversion and began to ruffle the ground and growl near his guarded escape route. His ears perked up immediately when he heard a scurry from below. He buried his snout into the hole and began to bare his teeth as wide as it would allow him to in the narrow tunnel.

On the other side, the creature made an appearance and scurried. But it froze for a moment, seeing the gargantuan golden tail of the other wolf. Wulfur raised his snout from the hole, hoping to see his son have the prey caught in his jaws. But instead, he saw the opposite. He gawped in disbelief.

"ELITE!" he bellowed.

Elite, currently with his nose close to the ground, jolted in surprise at his fathers' voice. His legs took a more aggressive stance, his tail flicking in the face of the muskrat. It squeaked and made a bolt toward the bushes. Still slightly stunned, Elite attempted to whip round and catch the muskrat by its' legs. But it was too late. The small innocent creature had evaded him and disappeared.

Wulfur approached his son, a face full of fire and his tail pointed out like a tightrope. Elite didn't cower this time. Instead, he looked at Wulfur with confusion.

"What was that?!" Wulfur growled. "Why weren't you watching that hole?"

Elite knew what he was distracted by. He knew his father would hate to hear about another shiny object. It would only sour his taste over the idea of using the duffel bags.

"I, er... the sunlight. It got in my eye, father."

"Blasphemy!" Wulfur exclaimed, his glare becoming more hostile. He felt a bit betrayed by his sons' actions. This wasn't the outcome he had hoped for. He had trained him for so long. How was he this incapable of focusing on a task that would reward him with food?

He walked up to Elite, fuming through his ears. "I see what you're looking at. Prioritising little shiny trinkets over your own hunger. Unacceptable. Face it, Elite. You wouldn't survive on your own."

Once again, Elite resisted from cowering in shame. He just stared back at Wulfur without any sign of regret. This made Wulfur stop moving too close to him. It looked like Elite had gained a lot of assertiveness since the human camp encounter. He would teach that boy an important lesson about being a wolf. He sighed angrily and turned his body away from Elite.

"You know what? Just stay here and play with your shiny things. I'm getting food, but don't think for a single moment that you are entitled to anything I bring back. You want food? Catch it yourself."

With that final punishing message, Wulfur walked slowly away from Elite into the thick, green fog of the forest. Elite watched, expressing very little about Wulfur's decision. He didn't acknowledge him either. He thought for a moment about all the progress they both had made. He taught himself how to climb a tree, whilst Wulfur taught Elite how to be a dominant male. Elite had modified the bags to fit him whilst maintaining a bit of agility. He learned how to catch fish. His father helped to heal the wound on his belly from that wretched log. And after all that, the tension between them was growing.

It didn't make sense to Elite why they couldn't just get along. Why was it difficult to maintain trust with the wolf he had spent all his life with? It dawned on him at that moment that Wulfur couldn't be the only wolf who'd be able to offer him guidance. Who could answer his questions. Truthfully.

Finally coming back to Earth, Elite raised an eyebrow at the half-buried artefact he had spotted a minute ago. He leant down and pulled it loose with his teeth. The object looked the same as those in his duffel bag: the golden round pieces with pictures of humans on them. The inscriptions were less clear on this coin, unlike the others. Not that Elite could read them anyway. He lowered himself to the ground and kept admiring the work of humanity. It fascinated him, but he had no wolf to share that fascination with. At least, no wolf who would listen to him about it.

It was quiet for a while. Elite found himself looking at the bag Wulfur had carried. Maybe there was some food in there left over from the humans. He got up to take a sniff at it for meat. But instead, he had his nose greeted by the scent of lavender and other aromatic herbs. He dug deeper and found the water container along with a few colourful plants. It was Wulfur's special mixture he had picked up a few days back. Elite looked around, checking if Wulfur had seen him snooping inside. Not a whisper. Elite then huffed angrily before beginning to take things out.

Wulfur, meanwhile, had neared the source of the pongy smell. A swamp would imminently be in his sights. But stopping him in his path was what he was looking for. A huge hole in the base of the tree, big enough to stick his head into. Through the musky air then came the attractive scent of fresh meat, that of which Wulfur recognised straight away.

He lowered his body so that he was crawling below the altitude of the entrance. The whiff of prey began to flood the area like a guiser does to spread its steam. Wulfur then silently pounced, only making noise after his skull cleared the gap and his shoulders bumped against the trees' exterior. The loud thud was accompanied by Wulfur's intense hunting growl. His beastly face caused the unlucky creatures inside the tree to squeal.

Wulfur pulled his head out with his jaw tightly locked on the leg of a marsh rabbit, still screaming in pain. The big wolf dragged it along the floor away from its' den. The rabbit had eyes that were struck with horror and little to believe in. Their exposed home wasn't safe after all. They had underestimated the size of the predator that could get in. *'What was a marsh rabbit family doing in the middle of the woods? They're normally out in open areas to see their predators for miles.'* Whatever the reason for their strange home, it only mattered that Wulfur had them at his mercy.

The unlucky rabbit was far from dead as only his leg had been ravaged. Wulfur continued to rear his way back to the area he had asked his son to wait. The old wolf saw Elite lying down, just observing the coin he had found, now accompanied by a few of the trinkets from inside the bag. Wulfur didn't look for long. He rolled his eyes and put a paw on the rabbits' body before releasing its' leg to make sure it still couldn't escape. With a couple of seconds left of pain to bear, the rabbit heard his killer speak to him, but with no connection to his language.

"The afterlife awaits you, rabbit. This was always going to be your fate," Wulfur chanted whilst staring directly into the rabbits' eyes.

In a savage movement, Wulfur latched his teeth on the rabbits' neck and tugged violently, causing a whip of blood to fly across the clearing. Traces of the deep red splattered on the ground nearer to Elite who, at this point, had turned to watch his father swiftly end the life of the mammal.

Wulfur turned to look at his son whilst the sound of smaller insects filled the void of the forest again. He picked up the lifeless herbivore and huffed at Elite before walking back toward his hunting ground.

Elite watched on. Wulfur had taken the rabbit with him. So, it seemed Wulfur was being serious about not feeding him. Elite quietly huffed back at him before returning his attention to the shiny objects. In front of him out of Wulfur's view, Elite had begun mixing the ingredients and had the water container by his side. He twitched, knowing he was about to try something his father might not forgive him for.

Back toward the tree where Wulfur had claimed the rabbit, he begun to sniff the air. An interesting scent caught his attention. A new animal? He navigated past the rabbit den which had been reduced to silence again.

A few foul and dead bushes later, Wulfur found himself ascending a steep overgrown root. It appeared to stretch like a limb across the earth, reaching the neighbouring tree. Wulfur carried his kill over the top and nearly slipped over the other side. His eyes met a marvellous sight. Right beneath him was the swamp. The bulgy, dirty water gave off a sickening aroma. But on the closest side where the swamp met the land, a big ball of fur, larger than Wulfur himself, was quietly snoring in the naturally formed dip beneath the giant tree root. A bear.

Wulfur's eyes widened with a mix of fear and consideration. A bear was a challenging prospect. On his own, it was checkmate and almost certain death. Wulfur backed away down the incline and turned to face the empty fog. He would have gotten Elite to assist with taking it down, but then he reminded himself of Elite's inadequate hunting abilities. Was he capable?

He shivered at the thought of Elite literally running away, not out of fear of the bears, but to depart Wulfur and leave him for dead. The way Elite had been behaving lately, and his ability to look beyond his father's orders meant that this possibility was far from unreal.

He sighed and then decided to return to Elite with no more food. A single rabbit would do for now. If he tried to hunt for more in proximity of the bear, he would surely alert them. But at least he knew of where to go if his son got his act together. Wulfur navigated back to the muskrat grounds where Elite was found indulgently licking the coin clean.

"Elite, what in the lands are you-"

His question was cut short when he saw his son's head spinning slightly, ears low and eyes dreary. That, along with the damp patch of his floral herbs and the water container now half-empty. "ELITE! You fool!"

Quickly thinking about his own safety, Wulfur tugged the rabbit up and over his snout, covering the nose and muffling his voice. He then pranced over to Elite and flimsily placed the container back into the bag with his paws. He shuffled Elite, making him stand up. The young golden wolf looked like he was going to lose his balance at any moment.

"Get moving, away from that!" Wulfur shouted, desperately trying to coax Elite out of the clearing.

Elite yawned loudly, staggering to the left, almost hitting a tree with his flank.

"Okay, father. Whatever you say."

Wulfur had a face of rage. Elite had just used up the herbs he had planned to use later. And now only half the water. At least he didn't ignite the fire. That would have been bad news for both. Wulfur held his breath, knowing the rabbit body was slipping from his snout. With Elite moving ahead, Wulfur tried to lift both bags by the teeth, his lungs straining to their limit. He followed the trippy Elite to another clearing nearby.

They both collapsed, Wulfur from the front ballast of his carry weight and Elite because of his trippy blurry vision and lack of energy.

"That was fun." Elite said, followed up with another yawn. Wulfur had a gargle in his throat. He attempted to speak like a teacher rather than shout at him.

"Was it fun? Great, Elite. Now I don't have my special herbs." Wulfur checked in the bag after getting up from the fall. There were still remnants of each herb at the bottom of the bag, along with the half-empty container and the matchbox, still in good condition. "Well, there's only a few bits left. How dare you, Elite. I should've known better."

Wulfur laid down on the ground and begun to pick at the limbs of the dead rabbit.

Elite kept changing his focus from the contents of the bag to Wulfur's dinner. His lips started to drool in sync with his rumbling belly. He withered his mouth open, exposing his teeth that were desperate for a good chow. He got up with his wearily limp bones and approached Wulfur slowly but confidently. Wulfur began to growl under his chewing, his ears making him aware of the nearing footsteps.

"Heh, I knew you were kidding about not feeding me," Elite said with a dizzy head. "C'mon, which bit don't you want?"

Wulfur slowed his chewing pace to a stop, flicking his eyes at Elite. He saw him acting playful. Wulfur knew his game and this guilt-trip talk was about to end.

"The bit I don't want is you anywhere near me. I told you, no food unless you catch it."

Elite tensed his shoulders at the response. He still fancied his chances.

"Alright, let me show you how I catch this," Elite scoffed. He then made a swift nosedive for the opposite end of the rabbit. Wulfur reacted immediately by stamping on Elite's nose. He whined sharply from the small hit of pressure on his sensitive cartilage. Wulfur had risen to his full height, abandoned the rabbit and tackled Elite to the ground, gripping the neck with his teeth. Elite let out a bark, indicating his sensitivity to the shock of pain. His head hit the ground with a thud as his dominant father pinned his torso with both front legs. He spoke a monstrous tone, his saliva gargling in his throat.

"I told you that you're not getting this food for free! You can't hunt for yourself and are trying to disobey me. Pathetic. Living on fish and plants for the rest of your life won't get you far."

Elite attempted to wriggle free and use his legs to push Wulfur off, but his old father was too heavy, let alone too strong. His face was sideways, grinding in the dirt as he opened his jaws to speak.

"But I'm your son. You should help to feed me. I'd get it if I was a stranger to you, but this is just silly," he replied with a panicked tone, trying to make a plea of innocence to his father.

Wulfur shook his son's neck, scarring the delicate skin under the golden fur. He began to shout at him.

"Don't you dare tell me what I'm doing is silly. You and your little obsession. You're delusional. I should have never let you steal the food from the camp. It should have been my job."

In the moments between tugs and pulls, Elite braved a smirk at his father, mocking him telepathically. With each strike of pain, Elite let out a playful huff and winced his eyes shut, continuing to argue back.

"Heh, nah. You would have been spotted easily. Also, *I* got those carry things. You would have never done that. I'm the reason we left that camp with so much food. You could never be that clever. It's all about just getting the food. You don't take a second to think about how to get it better than before."

Elite's light poke of the tongue afterward sent Wulfur's head over boiling point.

"THAT'S IT! I'LL TEACH YOU TO TALK TO ME LIKE THAT!"

He let go of Elite's neck and bit his left leg that poked the big wolf on his chest. Elite yelled in agony as his dew claw was impaled, along with the burial of Wulfur's teeth into his sensitive flesh. The golden male used all his body to try and wriggle loose of the grip, using his hind legs to kick upwards. But his tough father dodged them like he'd practiced this as a routine.

Wulfur then picked at Elite's limbs individually, leaving bite marks nearer to the paws. He spoke with fury between each bite.

"YOU DESERVE THIS, YOU LITTLE RUNT!... AND THIS!... YOU'RE A DISGRACE!... YOUR OBSESSION!... USING UP MY HERBS!... THINK YOU CAN BE A SLY FOX AROUND ME?!... GROW UP!"

Wulfur then got down to the hip of Elite's hind left leg and chewed even harder and longer than the rest, impaling Elite's biceps. Elite let out a feral cry for help, feeling hurt from every angle. He whimpered and whinged as he lay battered on the ground.

Wulfur kept going at his leg until he stopped suddenly. Wulfur's' ears were alerted to a nearby sound. A heart-curdling cry from the site of the rabbit den. Elite could barely raise his head to see, but Wulfur was immediately stood upright to anticipate the incoming threat. That sound was distinct, and Wulfur knew what it was given the direction it came from. He gasped and looked at Elite, now also able to look back at him. Wulfur showed signs of dread, hearing that the sounds were multiple threats.

"Elite, bears! We need to run."

Wulfur then turned an eye to the duffle bag duo and quickly ran to grab them. He slung them both over his head and began to dart for the forest exit, back to where they had come from. It was a bit of a trek, but he knew they had to keep moving.

"Elite, let's go!" he yelled as he ran away from the clearing.

Elite saw Wulfur in a blur make a run for the bushes. His head was on a tilt watching his father run away. Normally his father was courageous. He then turned to the source of the sound. He got up very slowly and shakily, feeling his muscles weak from the herbal essence and brutal bites dispensed to him by his father. Wulfur had already gone.

"Wait!" he yelled. "I can't... get up. Father!"

There was no reply, and Elite was left limping in the forest, still under a small amount of effect from the herbs he inhaled. The bears would certainly catch him like this. He looked around desperately for a way out. Around him were the trees, spots on the ground had his own blood marked and Wulfur had also left the half-eaten rabbit carcass behind.

Elite stopped and stared into the fog for a moment, trying to focus on the silhouettes of the two predators, one larger than the other. They appeared so vicious. The sound they made terrified him. He finally stopped moving and held still, hoping they would just go away.

Then Elite heard a caw sound. He opened his eyes to see that the bears had stopped advancing. A crow approached the rabbit corpse and began pecking at it. Was it the same crow again? Elite stood there for a while, trying to get his head back into working order.

Meanwhile, a long way ahead, Wulfur ploughed through bushes that appeared light enough to do so. He charged his way down the narrow path they had cut through before, finally slowing down when he could see the open pathway exposed from the forest depths. Those bags took a slight toll on his energy and had him breathing a little heavier than normal. As he took the last few steps out into the open air, he turned to see if Elite had caught up. There was no sign of the golden male.

"Elite! We made it out! We're going to that pack now, before dark," Wulfur bellowed with adrenaline still pumping through him. He had felt a surge of determination after being aggressive to Elite and then running from the bears. But the excitement soon faded as he realised that no reply was coming.

"Elite?" Wulfur called into the forest. He stood there and performed a light howl, calling for his son. "ELITE?!" He waited for a few moments, still exhaling loudly and panting with his tongue concealed behind his fangs. Nothing. No movement, no whisper, not even a scent. This was a problem.

Wulfur slowly allowed his ears to rest naturally whilst he closed his mouth. He blinked slowly, hoping that Elite would just appear late like before. The air was silent, but it told the story to Wulfur, at least the only result that seemed possible... was Elite dead? The old wolf let out a painful whine, feeling the hope drain out of him like an open tap. Yet his face showed the bare minimum of sympathy. *'If that runt hasn't survived, I will have to go to the den by myself,'* he thought.

His mind still racing with thoughts of domination and reputation, he trudged along, more slowly, heading East. He hoped his slow speed would allow for Elite to catch up to him... if he was alive. For the first time in years, Wulfur only had himself to travel with, the scent of his fallen son still lingering from the stray golden fur on the duffel bags. The old male kept his head low, and occasionally wandered with his eyes shut, thinking of what had happened. It had already gone dark, and his hopes of survival now laid with a seemingly peaceful pack. Wulfur moved in slow motion, maximising the time available to raise any sense of hope he had left. It may have been too late.

Chapter 7

It was the early hours of the morning, before the sun had come to rise from the East. The clouds were blocking almost all the light from the moon and had other plans of bringing light over the land. The mixture of greys and blacks in the sky ignited, making themselves known with an intimidating whirr of thunder.

Wulfur had walked so slowly that he hadn't even made the right-turn onto the field after the last few hours. He had found himself walking off-course with his mind constantly under stress. He had stopped a few times to think back to his time at the swamp as the events of last night started to haunt him.

He hated to admit it, but Elite grew to be a lot smarter than him, even if that wasn't anything to do with the hunting. His son was an ally to him, and Wulfur hadn't appreciated the way he thought out of the box. Now he was dead, Wulfur was without any wolf who would side him. He didn't know any acquaintances nor friends who would agree to help him. His only option was to join this pack and rest up, hopefully establishing a new plan at the same time.

He huffed angrily, more to himself than at anything else, as he veered right onto the open field. As the looney wolf had described, there was the pack entrance: an assortment of hedges with a gap through the middle just a little way across the South. They appeared to be trimmed, perhaps with wolves' teeth, to make a tidier shape and appear more obvious. Maybe a way to hide the fact it was indeed a wolf den. But this wouldn't deter Wulfur. He walked with more pace toward the entrance. As he neared, he could make out a silhouette of a wolf sat on guard there. Those dark clouds obstructed vision, but their scent remained potent.

The distant wolf turned his head in the direction of Wulfur, then jolted in surprise. Wulfur faintly heard a growl coming from them. He decided to show identical hostility by baring his fangs back.

"Hey! You're not supposed to come here!" the guard said.

"What do you mean?" Wulfur asked, casually strolling up to the guard.

"It means go away. No guests welcome," he replied.

Wulfur tried to contain his growl. He hinted his eyes past the guarding wolf.

"A little rat of yours said this place was welcome to guests."

"No, they didn't!" the guard spluttered. "I mean uh... what rat do you speak of? We have no rats."

This conversation was becoming silly and Wulfur soon put that fact to rest. As he closed in to the entrance, the wolf guard was Quade. Although Wulfur hadn't met him before, he was the mentor that Arvux was hanging out with yesterday, so Wulfur recognised some of the scent he had been suspicious of on arrival.

"That buffoon you call Arvy. Bit of a looney." Wulfur paused, noticing Quade divert his attention deliberately. "Seems like you know who I'm talking about."

Wulfur was going to push all the buttons on this persistent guard, for he could see how little he could cover up the truth. Whatever it took to get around him, he would do it.

"Not at all. The other way with you!" Quade instructed with a lump of worry in his throat.

"Listen here, mud snout," Wulfur snarled. "You got half a nests' worth of seconds to let me in or I'll-..."

"What's all the noise out there, Quade?" came a much smoother voice from inside the den.

"Alpha! Help me get rid of this wolf! It's him!" Quade cried out.

From around the den entrance came a tall grey wolf with a confident yet formal step in his stride. His arrival was soured by the pair of wolves in front of him growling at each other. Both Wulfur and Quade exchanged looks of disgust.

"Woah woah, hey. Calm down now," the Alpha wolf said, lifting his paw in reassurance. "What's going on here? We're all wolves here, can't we discuss matters like wolves?"

"Alpha! It's him!" Quade announced quickly. "He's part of the Goldfire. He's part of them!"

"Hm, so you say…" the Alpha responded, raising a paw and using it to gesture at the pair. "…but I only see a lone wolf here. Tell me stranger, are you here on your own?"

Wulfur hesitated, realising that his answer would now be completely different from yesterday.

"Yes. I have travelled by myself for a while and need a place of rest." He eyed the Alpha with a light tremble in his speech.

"He's lying!" Quade interrupted. "He's with the gold wolf. Those things on his back too. Alpha, please!" Wulfur growled at the brown-muzzled canine and Quade exchanged a snarl back at him.

"Enough, Quade," the Alpha ordered. "What's your name, traveller?"

"Ulfren," the timber male lied.

"Hm… well Quade, it seems as though the name doesn't match what we've been told."

Quade struck a paw forward, almost poised to protect the Alpha wolf.

"Alpha, I'm telling you this is no coincidence," Quade stated, his eyes twitching in response to his certainty. "I saw them earlier and he is a liar!"

"Right," the Alpha peered past Wulfur's shoulders. "But there isn't another wolf with him, so we have nothing to fear. Let him in."

The loyal mentor gawped at his Alpha. Had he gone insane? But who was he to disobey his master? Much to his disapproval, he nodded at the Alpha and backpedalled out of the way. The Alpha then exchanged the nod and suddenly put on a rather friendly, inviting face toward Wulfur.

"Well then, Ulfren. Welcome to the pack of unquiet dreams. We are quite the happy bunch. My name is Oslo, I am in charge here. Allow me to show you around. Follow."

Alpha Oslo took a wide turn, demonstrating how much room he had to move between the entrance for Wulfur to walk alongside. But instead, Wulfur decided to keep behind him. On the way through, Quade gave him an intimidating stare.

"Don't think you're getting away with this," Quade whispered. "If you try anything, I will tear you apart."

Quade let out an angry curdling growl but was quickly silenced by Wulfur snapping a bark back at him. The mentor wolf bounced back in fright. Wulfur then calmed down and smirked, seeing how weak and inferior the guard truly was. Wulfur knew he'd turn Quade into a meat pile if there was no governing pack to stop him.

Wulfur followed Oslo into the main clearing, where familiar sights greeted him: several leaf-covered dens, a prey pile heaped with meat and bones, and on the far side, a mother wolf weaning her pups.

The area did contain some interesting things, including rocks that had been carved on and decorated with flowers. There was a huge tree at the opposite end, with half of its' roots sticking out and over a small body of water. The gap was large enough to walk under and see the tree from the inside in more daylight. Wulfur also paid attention to the other wolves in the den as Oslo began to speak with him.

"So, you had met Quade before?" asked Oslo. "Sorry for the aggro, he was born a rogue so not the best upbringing." He kept his head slightly in front so that Wulfur could see him.

"Uh, no. It was a wolf named Arvy," the timber brute replied after hesitating over Quade's backstory. Wulfur started taking in the sights and doing some methodical planning in his head.

"Ah yes, he is a trainee of ours," Oslo proudly announced. "He's from The Eternal Rose in the far East. We are trying to make him a useful scout. Quade reckons he saw you. He's pretty good at hiding so it doesn't surprise me."

This made sense to Wulfur. He never saw another wolf when encountering Arvux, but he had smelt signs of other wolves nearby. And Arvux's origins, The Eternal Rose. Wulfur had heard of it being a bloodline locked kinship with a high reputation for wits and solution. It seemed fitting that Arvux was no longer a part of that family.

They continued to an open den where Jeeva, the trainee hunter, was resting. She looked up at Wulfur and dropped her jaw in disbelief.

"Here's the hunter trainee. Her name is Jeeva. Arvux's sister. Quade has trained her up very well and I am nearly ready to make it official."

Jeeva turned her head all kinds of directions, trying to spot her mentor. She knew he was on guard at the front and that he had vowed he wouldn't let this wolf in. She watched in silence as Wulfur was escorted to the centre of the clearing, where more wolves were gnawing on carcass bones. Oslo continued the tour.

"Here are a few spots for adults to sleep. Zavi and Fenn here are the lead hunters. Right next to them is a spot reserved for Jeeva, but you can use it for the time being."

The pair approached Zavi and Fenn. They both had a mixture of olives and greys in their pelts. Zavi was more rugged than Fenn, as if he were more battle-hardened. Oslo sat down next to the empty leaf pile and invited Wulfur to sit with him using his paw as a welcoming gesture. Wulfur did so. Another wolf, a female, quietly tapped her way toward Wulfur, her fur completely white and silky.

"Another guest, Alpha. May I?" she asked.

"Of course," Oslo replied. "Ulfren, this is Liara, the best healer in the land. Please allow her to check you for wounds."

Wulfur raised a paw to stop the white female from touching him. Without showing too much emotion, he gave a stern look to the healer. She had eyes of gleaming innocence, looking like she could charm any male into getting a health audit. Not Wulfur, he refused to be petted around with, let alone have the bags of goodies explored. His lifelines were inside, so he needed the other wolves to stay away.

"No, I think I will pass on that," said Wulfur.

"It's my job, sweetheart. I insist you let me check you," Liara responded.

"I said no," Wulfur declined, this time shifting her paw out of his face. "It would be a great help if you left me alone."

Liara frowned at the old male. She wouldn't let his comments offend her though.

"It's okay, Liara," said Oslo. "I'll take care of him."

The silenced healer turned away, allowing her tail to brush Wulfur's face. She stuck her nose up with a light huff and headed back to the den where the weaning mother laid with the pups.

"Well, I'm sure you'll get on better with the males here. I can count on Zavi and Fenn to keep you entertained," Oslo continued.

Wulfur had his eyes on the mother wolf as Oslo spoke to him.

"Who's that?" Wulfur pointed out.

"Oh, in the nursery?" the Alpha guessed. "That's Leyla. I am proud to have had pups with her. She had come from another pack. Well, I mean, she didn't come here by herself. I kind of... poached her out of there. Her bloodline will make my pack superior."

"Over what? Just other aspects?" Wulfur asked.

"The whole land, my friend," Oslo replied, placing a confident paw against Wulfur's shoulder. "The Wise Wolf promised me so."

"Follow the Wise Wolf!" Fenn bellowed from behind Wulfur. He shook off Oslo's paw and turned his head to see the pair of hunters bowing in an unusual fashion. They used a foreleg to cross over their chest and pointed their snouts downward. After that, Wulfur turned to see the mother wolf coughing between grooming the pups. Then he looked back at Oslo, unable to ignore that name.

"Who is he? The Wise Wolf? What does he do?" Wulfur suddenly felt an opportunity to get under the skin of the wolf who attacked him at the waterfall all that time ago.

"The Wise Wolf is a wolf that the Alpha of every pack in this region of land looks up to," Oslo explained.

"You mean aspects and kinships?" Wulfur hinted to the Alpha. This would really expose how much Oslo understood about the neighbouring territories.

"Of course not," Oslo chuckled. "Bah, all that kinship aspect stuff... bloodline this – paw leadership that. It's all baloney. A pack is tradition."

Alpha Oslo paused for a breath, seeing Wulfur lean back and hold his breath in dismay. "The Wise Wolf has assured me that every pack must have an Alpha. He lives on a cliffside in a cave of gems. We can visit him for advice and pack counselling. No wolf knows his real name for sure. Well, except his messenger. She's the wolf who delivers us the warnings from the Wise Wolf himself."

"And who is that?" Wulfur asked, his nose and ears twitching in irritation.

"Imelda," Oslo revealed. "She happens to have known him since young. They're both moon jumpers."

"And what messages has she delivered recently?" Wulfur gave Oslo an ominous look, whilst the Alpha kept his happy face on. He just smiled and stared back at the old male.

"The Goldfire," announced Zavi with a harsh tone, who was sat next to Fenn, both their chewable bones fully depleted of meat.

"Yeah," Fenn followed with, eyeing the bizarre cosmetics hanging from Wulfur's shoulders. "He speaks of a pair of land wanderers who turn packs into dust. Talon of gold and the other a bit like you, that traditional timber look."

Wulfur mellowed silently at the thought of the Wise Wolf. They had a messenger delivering warnings to packs. *'Very clever but rather lazy',* he thought. This also means that the Wise Wolf was spreading fear to these packs. Almost as if it paid into his favour. If only he had Elite with him be loyal enough to kill the Wise Wolf, then surely all packs would hear about the downfall and fear Wulfur instead. A plan so good he almost whined in shame under his breath, knowing that he didn't have the strength to do it alone.

"So, what are you going to do about the Goldfire?" Wulfur asked, hoping to get insight to the packs' preferred response to threats.

"Honestly, nothing," Oslo answered proudly, puffing out his chest. "If they did show up here, we'll just try to deter them, point their nose at another pack. And if that fails... pray."

Wulfur had mixed feelings about that answer. A good thing was that this pack seemed weaker than others. Almost laughably straight-forward to deceive. The problem Wulfur had was that this Alpha was either delusional, or something was up. The Wise Wolf may have given them a counselling that caused the whole pack to soften up. There was absolutely no reason to do that unless...

"That sounds a bit laid back, don't you agree? If I were the Alpha, I'd kill the Goldfire on sight," Wulfur explained.

"Like I said, we are a happy bunch," countered Oslo. "We live life to the happiest and we choose peace above anything else."

Wulfur had to hold himself back from laughing out loud. He swallowed his amusement like a frog eating a fly. This was blasphemy. A joke. He hadn't seen any group operate like this before in his life.

Oslo saw him flinch a smile but decided to continue rambling.

"Another pack... well, not really. A group further North of the river, Minnow's Paw, they are a bunch of cranky wolves who only find downtime when looking at the night sky. But during the day, their true savagery comes out. Their beliefs don't really come full circle with the ancestors. I think the Wise Wolf knows they're traitors to The Greater Ones and manipulated them to benefit me."

Wulfur twitched his ear. Minnow's Paw. Oddly familiar, but not down to his roots. But what Wulfur did know is that the wolves of Minnow's Paw didn't call themselves a pack and Oslo acknowledged this. And that the Wise Wolf had some say in their ways. It had to be false. The whole 'pack' idea was the real illusion. He kept that thought to himself though. There was no point in starting a debate over their beliefs when taking the pack down seemed so easy.

"Hm... okay," Wulfur acknowledged when Oslo paused for breath. This was when the Alpha got up and made a move toward his own den.

"I should return to my rock. I need to speak with Naito. You haven't met him. A trained scout and the prey pile guard. If you need anything, Ulfren, just ask the others. Don't touch the prey pile, it's for later when we feast. I think that covers everything. May the ancestors bless you."

Wulfur nodded then observed Oslo returning to his spot in the clearing, noticing yet another female camped there, waiting for him. They weren't the same wolf as the individual with the pups and that made Wulfur raise an eyebrow.

Before Oslo could reach the summit, he suddenly darted to the right and beneath the roots of the tree. Wulfur perked his ears up, hearing the Alpha mutter words down there, only being able to see his tail. Oslo then reappeared and walked back to his rock accompanied by a younger coffee-pelted male. It looked like the wolf who was in for a chat with the Alpha.

Then from the left, Quade dashed up to the rock and sat formally at the front. Wulfur could hear them from where he was sitting.

"I'm about to discuss important business with Naito. What do you want, Quade?" the Alpha demanded.

"Alpha, you really need to reconsider keeping this wolf in our den," Quade stressed through gritted teeth. From behind him, Wulfur grunted and frowned at Quade, similarly to how Elite frowned at *him* sometimes. Quade continued. "He's clearly dodgy. We should confiscate those carry things at the minimum."

Alpha Oslo gave a look of astonishment toward Quade. He spoke with a steely tone.

"Quade, I understand your concern, but the prophecy I have been given to follow does not give us an excuse to be rude to our guest. And as our lead scout, you should certainly stop making yourself look so foolish in front of him."

Right after that comment, a familiar looney wolf came bouncing up to Quade in excitement. "Ooh, hoo! Quade, I did it! I'm all cleaned up! And I didn't need to lick myself this time, hahaha!"

Oslo smiled at the bounding Arvux whilst giving a patient nod to Naito who waited on his side. "Now what job did I give you?" the Alpha asked to the mentor.

"To guard the entrance," Quade answered in frustration, trying to veer his head away from the jumping jester wolf.

"Good," the Alpha praised. "But take Arvux with you. He'll keep you company."

Oslo crept to the opposite side of the rock to have his discussion with Naito and the other female wolf. Quade inhaled a heavy breath and stomped his way to the entrance with Arvux close behind. Arvux stopped and noticed the familiar face of the wolf who pummelled him into the mud yesterday.

"Ooh! It's him! He was so friendly to me!" Arvux said, wagging his tail in delight.

"Shut up, Arvy," Quade snapped harshly.

They both trotted to the den entrance, Quade giving Jeeva a frustrated look. Wulfur watched as they both took a short glimpse back at him too. Wulfur knew he and Elite were the Goldfire, and that Quade and Jeeva were onto him.

It had become much quieter in the clearing, so Wulfur dropped the bags on his sleeping zone and got up to visit the mother wolf in the den. Up close, Wulfur noticed that she was rather sick, struggling for breath. The pups were chanting the songs of the ancestors to her, which struck Wulfur as a familiar puppyhood song.

"...stronger than lions, the land be ours to play in. Greater they were, they watch over us now, to find a purpose in myself and a reason to howl," they chanted in whispers.

"No dearests, it's 'ourselves'," the sick female croaked. "Remember, we are all a talon with the ancestors. Oh hello, dear. I'm Leyla. Are you new here?" she asked Wulfur when she saw him come in close. Wulfur stood over where she laid and gave his sincerest and kindest response.

"Yeah, I'm just travelling. You don't look so well."

"Hm, yes. I do feel rather poorly," Leyla admitted. Her voice remained fatigued and guttural. "I've been on meadow saffron to try and heal me. My mate Oslo is convinced it will help. The Wise Wolf told him to do it."

A young male pup bravely approached Wulfur, stumbling on his own paws and tail wagging gently.

"Pardon, big wolf..." he said with a light squeak. "...but mommy looks sick. Can you make her better, please?"

Wulfur glimpsed at the eager harmless pup. He was slightly amused at them for coming so close to a stranger to ask for help. He put together a fake smile for the youngster.

"Eh, she'll get better if your Alpha gives her the *right* medicine..."

His gaze then met back with Leyla, the smile disappearing and a grunt coming from below his throat. "...meadow saffron, huh... that's not good for you. If anything, it will make you lethargic. If you're his mate, then who is that other female up in his den?" he asked Leyla, his face boasting concern for the other wolf. The brave pup, meanwhile, cosied back up to his mother, a bit confused yet satisfied by Wulfur's response.

"Oh, pfff, she's nobody," Leyla said, using her paw to waver Wulfur's attention off the other female. "Her name is Freya though. She's the beta and I don't like her much. She's a bit jealous of me for birthing Oslo's pups."

Leyla lifted her head to lick her own paws, then proceeded to groom the pup closest to her chest as they quickly fell asleep from chanting the song.

"And as much as I love them, I had a better life in my old pack. It's just at the time I thought Oslo's deal was a good idea. He promised me eternal happiness. But I learned not long after we mated that he did it, not for love, but by guidance from a wolf living by himself in a cave near the waterfall."

"The Wise Wolf," Wulfur concluded.

"Exactly!" Leyla croaked, letting out a barrage of coughs afterwards. She aimed her breath at the ground to avoid rudely coughing on Wulfur.

Wulfur had heard enough. This was a messed-up pack. What was worse, it seemed other aspects in the region were also affected by this pack hierarchy trope. It was time to decide on his plans, especially how differently he would do so without his son at his aid.

"I'm going to head back. Your insight has been useful."

"My pleasure. May the Greater Ones watch over you," Leyla whispered before she laid her head on the leafy bed to rest with the pups.

As Wulfur returned to the designated spot he could sleep in, he saw the coffee-pelted wolf sniffing at the surface of his bag. It was Naito. Wulfur snarled at him to grab his attention. Naito looked up and gave a curious impression.

"Hey. I couldn't help but notice these interesting objects. What are they exactly?" the young male asked. His voice was rather ratty and snarky.

"They are none of your business," Wulfur replied with a stern tone. "Get away before I make you sorry."

Naito jumped backward off the leaf pile and kept his tail low to pose as little threat to Wulfur as possible.

"Did you get these from humans? I collect stuff like this. Maybe I could help-"

Naito's voice faded away seeing Wulfur continue walking past the bags and up toward him. Wulfur's height was intimidating with a stance so fierce unlike Naito.

"Eh, heh... okay, wuh- Ulfren. Point taken. I'll see myself away," the coffee-pelted adolescent teased and made a light dash for the prey pile.

Naito got there and sat by the stash with a confident stance, checking left and right of himself for any listeners. Wulfur could tell that Naito took his guarding job seriously, despite the interest in his carry gear. The old male turned around to the bags and decided to rest on top of them, hoping that no wolf pinched them whilst he wound down. For the first time in months, he took a nap in the safety of a pack.

Chapter 8

The eerie grey cloud cover had dispersed, allowing the afternoon light to beam over the pack grounds. Grasshoppers chirped between the thick grass walls that led to behind the giant tree. The clearing felt alive with the sounds of birdsong from the nests and pups at play.

Wulfur laid in a prideful position with his head held high, and tail relaxed. He was mostly familiarising himself with the clearing, even after Oslo gave him the tour. But his posture did not reflect well with what he was thinking. His eyes might have told a better story as he had to, every now and then, snap out of a daydream. At least if he looked like he was naturally pondering, no wolf would be suspicious.

Now was the time to consider what he would do... without Elite. He sighed, feeling liability creeping up on him. So, his actions got Elite killed. So what? Wulfur grunted after every exhale. The thought of his blameworthiness for Elite being gone forever loomed over him. He always knew Elite was not capable of anything beyond fishing and fetching herbs. His poor combat abilities and hunting standards would have seen him at the mercy of a rogue wolf in the future anyway.

His eyes scoped the entrance, hearing a few friendly greetings between other pack members. A few moments later, an unfamiliar female wolf stepped carefully into the clearing. She had a coffee pelt, just like Naito, only it had just the base colour with a dabble of white on the chest and a dark liver nose. She did not walk far before Alpha Oslo approached her with more pace and joy.

"Sapphina!" Oslo greeted, lightly wagging his tail. "You're back from scouting. Hope your entire journey was safe."

The female scout frowned at her Alpha.

"Um, no, actually..." Sapphina began. Her cold tone sounded strangely comforting to Wulfur who was listening in.

"...you sent me South to check the human advancement..." Sapphina started to breathe wearily, as if she were about to howl in mourning.

"...why didn't you send Naito?!" she whinged.

Oslo tried to keep his smile in front of Wulfur. He spoke through gritted teeth but with friendly eyes.

"Woah, calm girl. Don't embarrass me in front of the guest," he said, leaning his head toward where Wulfur laid. "Tell me what happened."

"I got only as close as I dare could," Sapphina explained. "I could see the fire. I tried to keep near, but a coyote...it attacked me. We got spotted. Horrible things them coyotes. I had never run so fast." The seasoned scout hung her head low in shame. Oslo observed her pose and kept smiling and slowly unclenched his teeth.

"You should've sent Naito," she continued, "I don't care what the Wise Wolf told you to do! My other kinswolf can tolerate all those human things and would've done a better job than me!"

Sapphina began to whimper, feeling in the wrong for being so afraid. Oslo knew that without the guest here, he easily could have punished her for being so negative about his decision as the Alpha. Obeying was mandatory, and choosing to contradict that decision was sanctionable.

The Alpha simply smiled and wavered her to go under the hideout beneath the tree roots.

"Get yourself some water," Oslo calmly ordered. "I'm sure Naito will be happy to see you."

The female nodded woefully at her Alpha then trudged with her head low toward the tree. As Oslo ominously retreated to his high rock, Wulfur noticed on his right that both Zavi and Fenn were listening to that discussion. Zavi huffed.

"Argh, those ravik coyotes," he snapped, slowly turning his head to both his brother Fenn, and Wulfur. "If I so much as find that pest who hurt Sapphina, I'll snap them in half!"

"Yeah!" Fenn agreed, grooming his own paw. "And then she might like you."

Zavi gave a silent snarl at his brother, his ears heating up. Fenn returned the snarl with a little giggle. Wulfur stared blankly at the entrance, ignoring them both.

"Well, I stand a better chance than you," Zavi taunted. "You'd snap in half just feeling her weight on you."

"Hah," Fenn scoffed at his brother. "And if she was with you, you'd accidentally suffocate her in your musky scruff!"

"Nah, no way!" Zavi exclaimed. Then he paused to think. When he had a resolve, he lifted a paw, pointing with it at Wulfur. "Hey, Ulfren! You can tell us. Which of us will be the better mate for Sapphs?"

Wulfur kept his chin rested on the ground, not bothering to look at nor reply to Zavi. In the silence, the olive-pelted brothers slowly transmuted their expressions into disappointment.

"Aw, I don't think he's playing along," Fenn whispered. "That means I win."

Zavi stood up feeling well rested and shook his pelt.

"No it doesn't. I'm going hunting," Zavi declared. "Need to fulfil my duties this moon."

"Yeah, me too," said Fenn. "I'm bored out of my head here. We'll miss the pack feast, but whatever food we find out there, it's ours!"

The pair walked formally away from where Wulfur laid. *'A bit of peace and quiet, perhaps,'* the timber male thought. He could continue to think of his plans here at the den. Without Elite, it was unlikely he'd be able to destroy it.

Maybe he could ascend the ranks. Prove his worth as a warrior, outperforming the hunters. Then maybe, when he acquired maximum trust, he could frame the Alpha for dishonesty, breaking up the pack! Or he could just kill him out of pack grounds and write it off as an accident. That thought made him smile. The opportunity to assassinate a superior wolf was extremely tempting. Especially this Alpha. Oslo was way too laid back. He'd probably cower if Wulfur threatened him enough. He *was* threatening.

It made him smirk, knowing Oslo had no idea he was the notorious killer camping in his den. That day when Wulfur would triumph, it would be grand. Any surviving wolves would be at his mercy. They'd have to agree to fight and kill the Wise Wolf with him. They would have no choice! It would be his ultimate victory!

This plan was coming together nicely in his head. No wolf here looked as intimidating or sounded as cunning as the Wise Wolf. These easy targets had barely any backbone to their structure. He imagined the satisfaction he'd have watching the other wolves beg for their miserable lives.

By this point, Wulfur had closed his eyes, feeling his own weight relax on the duffel bags. The black magic weapon was stowed under his rear-right leg and was bulging against him. He felt a tingle but wasn't sure if it was coming from the bags. An urge inside him came around to proceed with the new objective once he had rested up.

His little snooze ended abruptly when Wulfur heard yapping and growling coming from the entrance. A few of the other wolves, including Liara and Alpha Oslo, took notice and began to walk down there. Wulfur raised his head, his ears making sense of the rustling and barking. They were in conflict. Wulfur used his nose. Immediately after a concentrated sniff, his eyes widened. *'No way. It couldn't be.'* He rose up from his resting spot, ruffling the bags with his feet and cantered over toward the commotion with a whirring ache in his gut.

As he approached the corner, Wulfur heard Quade shout at the unknown opposition.

"No! Get lost! You're not welcome here!" he had said as Wulfur neared Quade's poised tail.

"You guard the entrance?" said the other. "Must be tough being the only wolf in the group whose biggest threat is a rabbit invasion."

That voice. Wulfur turned the corner seeing exactly what he had heard. It was Elite! Elite was alive. Wulfur gawped under his breath seeing his son again, still with a few wounds from when he beat him into the dirt.

Arvux was lingering to the side watching the golden wolf challenge Quade.

"Ooh! Fight fight fight fight fight!" Arvux chanted at them.

Quade was fuming, looking like he was going to pop a blood vessel.

"Why you! I'll kill you!" he raged.

"Elite!" Wulfur yelled, his jaw unable to close from the surprise.

The golden male winced his eyes over toward his gobsmacked father. Hearing Quade threaten to kill Elite, Wulfur barged into him. Quade stumbled into Arvux's side, saving his fall. Oslo had approached the scene along with Liara, who suspected there probably was a wolf in need of healing.

"Stop it, mud snout! That's my son!" he snarled at Quade, who had no confidence to snarl back after earlier and instead kept close to Arvux. Wulfur exhaled out of his nose in disgust and turned to face his son once again. His voice softened. "I thought you were dead."

Elite kept his teeth on show whilst observing all these new wolves accompanied by their strange smells. He eyed them all before returning the look to Wulfur.

"I thought I was dead too..." he grunted, lowering his eyebrows and flaring his nostrils. "...but look at me. I'm fine." Elite murmured slowly, taking a step toward his father with his neck stretched forward. "You left me on my own."

Wulfur hesitated, hearing Elite speak loudly about what he did. This was awkward. His son never made things easy. But surely, he remembered the directive. Why would he say anything to put them both on the line?

Oslo stepped between them to lighten the mood.

"Aw, isn't that nice? A reunion. Come. You must be exhausted, um... desert traveller?" Oslo wondered, taking an eyeful of Elite's impressive golden pelt.

Elite felt the need to step back from the precarious grey wolf.

"Hey, back off, numbskull!" he snapped.

Wulfur gave a nervous laugh toward the Alpha, also signalling Elite to remain silent with a draw of the paw across his own neck.

"Ha, boys, eh?" he poorly joked through his clenched teeth. "They always have an attitude."

Elite frowned hard enough to scrunch all his face muscles at once. Wulfur dropped his facial act to make sure Elite took notice. It would hopefully give Elite some comfort.

"Yes, now let's head back to the main clearing," Oslo ordered. "You all must be hungry."

"Alpha?" Quade asked with his bones stiff like stone.

"Not now, Quade," Oslo replied.

"Alpha! You can't let this wolf in too! I'm trying to do my job!" he bellowed.

"Well, you should try not being so awful at it! Ha!" the Alpha cackled to himself making moves into the den, followed by Wulfur and the stroppy Elite.

Quade remained frozen against Arvux, thinking about what had just happened. What was he doing being loyal to his Alpha when he wasn't talking sense anymore? His patience went string-thin when the jester wolf decided to speak.

"Hey mentor Quade. Why is it that whenever a stranger appears you must foul yourself?"

This made Quade move to check under his legs in case he did have an accident.

"Haha! Made you look!"

Arvux laughed as he dashed for the way into the den, leaving Quade bewildered by the Alpha's decision and, in a way, humiliated. The alpha was told about the Goldfire and how to avoid them. This was clearly them! What else did the Wise Wolf say to Alpha Oslo? Quade's head took a turn to the edge of the fields. After that small thought, he began to trot away from the pack, heading down a route across the clear grounds and into the forest. He kept his nose down, confidently following a familiar scent and avoiding the path that the hunters, Zavi and Fenn, had taken.

Back in the den, Wulfur's questioning of Elite's survival still lingered in his mind as he sat firmly on the spot he had been given earlier today. Elite approached without even glancing up at his father. After Liara and Arvux went back to their rest areas, Oslo came up to them both and began speaking about the pack again.

"And what might be your name, young traveller?" Oslo asked enthusiastically.

"Elite," he replied hesitantly.

Oslo tried to process the meaning behind that name. It wasn't like anything he had heard before.

"Elite? Hm, quite unusual. Well, I'm Oslo, the Alpha of this den. Welcome to the pack of unquiet dreams. We are quite the happy bunch."

He beamed at Elite and Elite returned an eerie expression that might have read "go away." Wulfur sighed angrily behind them, not wishing to hear the whole tour again.

"Over there we have our trainee hun-", Oslo was stopped by Wulfur moving between them.

"That's enough," Wulfur intervened. "I will tell him the pack details. You go and be your Alpha self."

Normally, an interruption like that was punishable in the pack, but these wolves were simply passing guests rather than actual pack members. Oslo decided to nod at the strong timber male.

"As you wish, Ulfren. May the ancestors bless you."

Elite gave a disgusted look to his father as they both sat in front of the duffel bags.

"Ulfren? What kind of-", Elite was hushed by his father who had put a paw up against his nose.

"Be quiet, Elite," Wulfur whispered, making sure the Alpha had walked away far enough not to hear them. "That's who they think I am. Now, how did you survive the bears?"

The golden male held his frown whilst his father waited for an answer. *'What was wrong with him?'* Wulfur thought, seeing how lifeless his eyes were. Wulfur then slowly navigated his paw to the side and padded his son on the cheek vigorously.

"Elite! Tell me!" Wulfur said, a bit louder this time.

Feeling the harsh tapping against his skull, Elite made a movement in his eyes after holding them still. He focused on his father and spoke with a light tone, suppressing any deeper feelings he had.

"I, uh... the rabbit carcass you left behind. I threw it at the bears. Distracted them long enough to get away."

"Really?" said Wulfur with a hasty sniff toward Elite's fur pelt. "And you didn't come after me?"

The golden male lowered his head and tilted his ears downward.

"I lost your scent. I decided to hide. All night. I only found your scent after retracing my path into the forest. But I had to come back. I'd die out there. I can't survive on my own, remember?"

That last comment made Wulfur blink in sympathy. He withdrew his paw slowly from Elite's face and looked around him to check for listeners. A part of him wanted to apologize to his son for abandoning him in the first place, but Elite's reassuring loyalty struck energy into the old male. His face grew with ambitiousness. Now that Elite was here, Wulfur could execute the original plan.

"Whatever. Now listen up, Elite," he began.

Elite let out a moan of frustration, fuelled by his distaste on pack culture. Wulfur continued.

"The Alpha is not strict, but something isn't right about him. About the whole pack. The Wise Wolf seems to have shaped their routines to make them vulnerable. I want to know why so much trust is placed on the Wise Wolf. But they know about us, Elite."

Wulfur's voice became a whisper. "You and me, we're known as the Goldfire. The Wise Wolf has a messenger telling other aspects about us."

Despite everything he was conflicted with, Elite intently listened as he had always done for his father. He didn't understand how packs truly operated as Wulfur had kept him hidden from these cultural practices. It was clearer to him that not knowing too much aided Wulfur's cause.

"Every wolf in the pack can come and eat now. Pups' priority please!" Oslo called out from the rock.

Elite and Wulfur exchanged looks at this free opportunity to fill up on their bellies. Wulfur huffed. Maybe they did need time to plan for this.

"We should go over there and try to join in," Wulfur suggested.

Elite eyed the crazy number of wolves heading up to the prey pile, including the three little pups. Then he looked back at his father.

"Uh, sure. I guess your idea can wait."

As they began walking, Elite heard footsteps behind him. He turned to see the coffee-pelted male looking at the bags.

"Hey, back off!" Elite said toward the snarky scout.

Wulfur saw this too and stood on guard, making sure Naito didn't attempt to take anything from inside the bags.

Hearing the golden male's voice, Naito looked at Elite with a gentle smile and a convincing pair of affectionate eyes.

"Woah there, handsome. Your father was very protective of these things. Mind if I ask what's in them? I do collect human artifacts you know. They are... fascinating."

"That's right. Keep your nose out," the golden wolf snapped. But then he lowered his head, taking momentary glimpses at the loot he was protecting. "Oh... you do?"

Naito's voice had neutralised Elite's snarl. Why didn't he have the capacity to argue with it?

He kept vigilant with the bags as he'd always prevent strangers from coming near him. But after visualising the other wolf and hearing him speak, Elite wasn't sure about writing him off as just another pack member.

"Yeah!" Naito said proudly. "You like them too? No wolf in this pack appreciates these things."

Elite shuffled his paws in front of the male. He felt interested in him. But it was for the human stuff, right? As the scout closed in, so did Wulfur from behind.

"I'm Naito. I got my name from the humans."

Elite turned to his father with a very blank expression and held his breath. After a moment, Elite realised Wulfur wasn't going to stop him. He turned back to Naito and kept his head low. He spoke nervously.

"My name is from the humans too. It's Elite. It's apparently shown on this carry thing."

"Oh? Let me see," Naito said, heavily intrigued. He wanted to take these bags to his hideout and examine them. But before he could get a closer look, Wulfur shoved his teeth between the pair and bit into the handles of both bags. Elite remained silent, watching his father intrude.

"Oh no you don't, pipsqueak," Wulfur said, his nose aiming at Naito's head. "These are coming with me." With that, Wulfur stormed off with the duffel bags toward the gathering, leaving Elite and Naito by themselves.

"How rude," Naito commented, coming in much closer to Elite with a prickle of interest running through his fur.

"Don't try to challenge him," Elite replied. "You said you collected human objects?"

"I do!" Naito answered, his tail twitching in delight. "I have loads of stuff!"

Elite looked around for help from his father. He wasn't here. He was on his own... but not entirely. He was with this other male. Elite felt his weight shift, noticing more of Naito's eye detail and his flicking whiskers below the nasal cartilage.

For a moment it was silent, and the pair had a fair exchange of glances. Naito's ears were heating up and he raised a paw behind his neck, feeling pressured to maintain eye contact. Elite was confused as to how he felt about observing the other male this closely. These senses tingled him all over and he didn't know why. Elite's paws tensed as Naito opened his mouth to speak, watching his teeth and tongue gesture at him.

"Heh, uh... well, I'm hungry. You must be too. Let's go join your father to eat some of the stash," Naito suggested.

"Yes," Elite replied formally with a little wobble in his throat. "Maybe afterward, you could show me what you got?"

The coffee-pelted male could barely contain his excitement. He felt an inner desire to impress this wolf. This golden male was genuinely interested in his discoveries. Naito yipped happily, bopping into the air with just the muscles in his toe beans.

"I'd like that. And I'd love to know more about you too. Let's go before the scraps are gone."

Elite gave a polite nod and made his way up to where his father had started feasting. Naito stood there for a moment, feeling his heart rate increase whilst watching Elite's tail tip swing low like a pendulum as he walked off. Briefly, Naito looked under the tail to see the faint wounds on Elite's hocks. Perhaps he'd ask about them later.

Naito followed behind from a distance, keeping his smitten face out of sight from the other pack members. He wouldn't sit with him for the food, just in case his big father tried to scare him off. But Naito felt warm towards Elite. Was it just the prospect of having an equal human artifact-loving buddy, or was it something more? Once Elite was sat with Wulfur, Naito made a playful stride to the circle with wolves he was familiar with. They made their ancestral prayers before devouring the plentiful nutrition accumulated by the pack.

Chapter 9

Darkness crept over the land, shrouding the flowers of spring under a blanket of shade. Inside the packs' camp, the feast was over, half the prey pile remaining on reserve. Most of the pack had decided to relax. Zavi and Fenn had returned with some fresh meat and Liara was chatting with the den mother, Leyla. Elite and Wulfur laid next to each other, licking their lips after that hearty meal.

"See? I told you the Alpha would let us have some," said Wulfur. "Yeah, a few other wolves looked at us like we would try something, but I assure you they trust us. Elite?"

His son didn't reply. Elite licked his dew claw and then used it to brush clean his ear. He fidgeted slightly when the scars rubbed on him. The scars Wulfur had marked him with. Hearing no response, Wulfur looked ahead at the Alpha's rock and could see the tails of Oslo and Naito behind it. *'Them both sure do enjoy having discussions,'* Wulfur thought. He decided to whisper at Elite with his idea.

"Elite, listen. That Naito boy who was trying to snoop at our stuff..."

Hearing the name of the wolf who made the fur on his neck tingle, Elite stopped washing himself and slowly turned to his father's intense glare.

"...he's the guard of that food stash. I want you to distract him when you can. As soon as I know you have him out of sight, I will stash most of that food into the carry things."

Elite gave him a deadpan look, his brows once again tempted to furrow.

"So, I'm back to distraction duty?" he mumbled.

"Yes," Wulfur replied in a husk of breath. "Keep quiet though. You're much better at doing that. Besides, I saw you both giving each other the look. Chances are he'll trust you more than me."

Elite allowed his lips to feather about whilst giving a gaze of uncertainty toward his father.

"The look? What do you mean by that?" The golden male asked with a forming lump in his throat.

"I mean he likes you," Wulfur answered quietly. "So just act interested in his... human things. Then go with him to that spot under the tree. That's where he goes to sleep, I think. Talk to him, do whatever you want. Just hold him long enough for me to get away from the stash. And when I come to get you, we ditch him and leave the den. Got it?"

There were a few seconds of total silence in the clearing. Wulfur checked around for any others listening in. His son stared at him blankly, trying to process what his father was speaking about. At first, the idea seemed rather normal to Elite. But he would be distracting that coffee-pelted male who also shared an interest in synthetic objects. He felt a little buzz in his brain each time he pictured Naito's face. Elite was regularly accustomed to playing the distraction role in other aspects, and even then, he never felt any chill or tingle in his bones over who he was deceiving. But Naito was different.

"And if you get caught?" Elite slowly croaked, his ears pivoting downward like falcon wings. He peered up at his fathers' more intimidating face, knowing that he asked this question a lot.

Wulfur observed the look in Elite's eyes. He could tell that Elite was interested in Naito. He had led Elite so blindly through life and, as a result, other wolves were teaching him lessons before Wulfur could do so himself.

Wulfur shook the thought off by wavering his head left to right, then giving his neck a stretch. He got up slowly, uncovering the duffel bag he had been resting on. Standing on his fours, he gently gripped the zipper and pulled it lightly, giving him just enough space to poke his snout into the interior. He then popped his nose through the gap and grabbed the matchbox with his teeth. Wulfur was slow to raise it, his retinas darting to the corners of his eyes, checking for eavesdroppers.

"I will use this," he whispered through tightened jaws. "Everything will burn. You'll know when to run."

Elite's eyes widened at the sight of the box. Adding Wulfur's description, the golden male realised that the little box was going to make fire. Elite didn't have the attention span to ask how it worked. For now, he would take Wulfur's intentions for granted. More to his sense of unease, betraying Naito was looking to be the difficult part.

"Hey, Elite!" came a familiar voice, close to the large tree.

The call for his name made Elite jump slightly. Wulfur quickly concealed the matchbox inside the bag. It was Naito, hot on approach. Wulfur snarled at him, displaying his lack of approval for the surprise. Elite, on the other paw, looked over at Naito with a straight face. The golden male struggled to keep it that way, seeing the snarky wolf skip toward him. Naito ground to a halt, almost bopping Elite on the nose with his own.

"What do you want?" Wulfur asked distastefully.

"Father, let me handle this," Elite suggested to him.

Wulfur looked at Elite with momentary disbelief before he paused to think. The whole plan meant it was Elite who had to do the talking with Naito. Wulfur would prefer that Elite distracted another male by flirting whilst he stole the food. Not the other way around. Yuck.

After Wulfur gave Elite a slow, yet uncomfortable nod, Elite turned back to the energetic scout.

"Um... Naito, right?" Elite enquired.

Naito spoke rather loudly, alerting his kinswolf, Sapphina, just a few yards to his left.

"That's right, handsome. Did you want to see my collection now? You're going to be super surprised! I know us wolves have limits on our exposure to man, but I like breaking the rules." He beamed at Elite, noticing his continued interest after getting close to touching noses and complimenting his looks.

That was when he heard Sapphina speak from where she rested.

"Yeah, the rules of Tail Master," she taunted. Also hearing this, Jeeva giggled from the trainee resting spot on the other side.

Naito swung his head to the left and then to the right, feeling a sense of shame lurking on his head. He tried to argue back.

"That game still takes guts," the scout replied, unamused by the pair of females who were quietly laughing at him from different angles. A very light snarl escaped Naito's mouth.

Elite hadn't taken much notice of Sapphina or Jeeva. He seemed transfixed on Naito, looking at every twitch on his face. Wulfur, however, could see that Naito's view on human involvement was greatly frowned upon by his other packmates.

Finally, Naito returned to giving attention to the golden male, still within touching distance. His eyes flicked momentarily to see Elite's not-so-pleased father, giving him a wary frown.

"Anyway, why don't you come to my hideout, Elite? I want to show you my things."

"Uhm, sure," Elite responded cautiously, getting up to grab the heavier duffel bag, only to feel his tail be pinched by his father again.

"No, because it's too early," Wulfur snapped, hoping Elite would take the hint that he was speaking about their little heist. The old timber male needed as many wolves in the den as possible to be relaxed. Evidently, the pack was still active and social, except for Leyla who had fallen asleep with the pups. The bag Elite was grabbing also contained his weapon.

"You're not taking the carry thing with you, either."

"Father..." Elite said, turning to face Wulfur. "The stuff inside will surely keep us busy."

He gave his father a wink. Wulfur thought for a moment and then realised that Elite's idea worked. But he needed the matchbox as a backup plan. He sighed and opened the bag up again, his teeth getting a little bit caught up in the torn fabric. He reached in with his head and grabbed the little white box, carefully concealing it in his jaws from Naito's view, and placed it inside the other bag. He also grabbed the half-empty water container and moved it away. Other than a strip of deer hide and the mixture of herbs Wulfur had exclusively kept separate, it was empty, ready for food. Wulfur could afford to use the space inside to hide the matchbox.

"Alright," Wulfur said, nodding slowly. "Just make sure you bring it back. It will be an hour before I need you. Just listen out for me. And you, dusty boy. Don't you have a job to do?" he asked, eyeing the prey pile.

Naito widened his eyes with a low growl after Elite's father called him that. But he was silenced rather pleasantly seeing Elite pick up the bag with all the human-designed goodies inside. It made him shiver in delight hearing Elite so eager to join him. He was going to find out what was inside the bag soon, and that made him beam at the pair.

"Ahh, that can wait. Don't worry, Ulfren," Naito said to Wulfur. "I will keep him safe."

Naito gave the old timber male a snarky grin before breaking eye contact and turning toward his hideout.

Wulfur didn't feel keen on Naito, like how he wasn't keen on any wolf here. He knew that if Elite's distraction was successful and they escaped with the food, Naito would be in a lot of trouble. It would wipe that snarky smile off his face for sure. Elite was much larger and smarter than at the time of their encounter with the Wise Wolf, so he was more than capable of pulling this off.

The pack was also a lot more laid back than many of their previous successful raids. Oslo clearly wasn't fit for the Alpha role. That was the only anomaly that struck Wulfur by surprise. If it weren't a falsity, this would be the easiest steal of his life. He took another glance inside the remaining bag, seeing the leftover herbs from Elite's shenanigans back at the swamp. Then he looked up to

Elite and gave him a subtle nod before he lowered, pretending to rest.

Watching his father settle on the grass, Elite slowly blinked, taking a moment to grasp that he was playing that distraction role with Naito now. He could not allow for this to go wrong, not after all his training and promise. He had to impress Wulfur now, no matter the odds.

After picking up the bag, Elite approached Naito who was bounding slowly over to the tree. It was even larger up close. A pair of wolves could stand nose-to-tail inside of it.

Naito padded his way down a steep dip which led to a muddy passageway. Elite took down the slope a lot more steadily, knowing Naito likely navigated here many times before. The path followed under the tree's exposed roots. They appeared to connect to the dirt beneath the body of water, with gaps wide enough for wolves to usher through.

As Elite followed Naito further, he felt surprisingly warm under the protection of the tree. Looking on his left, there was a small drop that led to a mushy pond, filled with lily pads, reed grass and pondweed. The golden male could hear frogs croaking down there. It felt somewhat unsettling, yet serene.

To his right, where Naito had stopped to face him, was a sight to behold. His nest was made of a strange soft material. It was placed directly under the tree. Surrounding the nest were many unusual things. Some chrome utensils were piled up in a corner, a few round and some sharp. Next to those was a strange white block with buttons and a short metal piece sticking out the top.

On the other side of the nest, smaller coin-like objects, like those that Elite discovered, caught his attention vividly. They were rested in front of some flat green paper stacks.

Naito enthusiastically itched for Elite's reaction.

"Whoa..." the golden male said, dropping the bag out of his mouth in awe. "What is all this?"

"I don't normally have guests, so I'm not sure how to summarise it," Naito admitted. "But I figured you might already understand a couple of things."

Elite kept his eye on the gold coins as Naito spoke. They gave off a shine that kept him looking. Naito noticed where Elite's snout pointed.

"Oh, you like those?" Naito asked, slowly approaching his new friend.

"Yeah, um... I have some like these in this carry thing," Elite said, returning a nervous smile with his ears pinned outward.

"They call it a bag. Ooh, can I see? Can I?" he pleaded in eagerness. Naito resisted the temptation to help himself to the contents of the bag.

"Yeah, hold on, let me..." Elite let his sentence drift into silence as he carefully pulled the zipper all the way across. He placed a paw in to feel for the golden pieces. As he searched, he looked up at Naito who sat there rather still, eyeing Elite more than the bag.

The golden male furrowed his brows, his own curiosity drowning in a pool of concern.

"Are you okay?" Elite asked Naito.

The coffee-pelted scout squeezed his shoulders and tried to suppress his dramatic grin.

"Yeah, I'm fine. I just like what I see, you know?"

"Not really," Elite replied with a light furrow of his brows, finally locating a coin buried under a few feathers. "Here."

Elite lifted out his paw with the coin wedged in between his frontmost claws. Naito got up to look more closely. The shine made his eyes glow.

"Do you know what these are for, Elite? May I?" Naito asked, holding out his paw.

"No idea," answered Elite, giving a light nod before lending the coin to him. The touch of his paw was soft and passive. Elite took notice of Naito's retracted claws that were out of harm's way.

"Well, I can tell you," Naito said proudly. "The humans use these items to trade for... well, *other* items. Same for those green things. They're exchanged for food, water, shelter. Even for stuff less critical for survival! Look over there."

Naito pointed with his right paw at the big white block with the antenna. Elite kept his head low, trying not to forget his mission. But it was proving much harder than he anticipated. The human artifacts plus Naito's charm were causing Elite to think and feel differently. He needed to remain focused.

"That device," Naito began. "I got no idea what it's for. But you can hear humans speak through it when you press the right buttons. I don't know if it still works, but if you're a human, you need a lot of those gold pieces to trade for it. You get the device, and the trader gets your gold. Fascinating, isn't it?!"

Elite gawped slightly at how much this snarky wolf knew about these mysterious objects.

"Yes, that is... kind of strange," he said. "I couldn't imagine wolves ever needing such a silly thing to swap for food. Well, perhaps you could work out what this does..."

Naito looked back over at Elite, seeing him put both paws around something inside the bag. Something big. His eyes widened with intrigue as Elite pulled out the black magic weapon.

"Whoa! Oh my..." Naito placed the coin on the ground as he was lost for words, even rubbing his eyes, worried that he was imagining things. "This... this is a..."

The scout shuffled nearer to Elite, almost sitting right next to him to admire from the same angle. He leant closely for examination, feeling the fur on his thigh brush the golden male's leg.

"Elite... how did you get this?"

Elite hesitated for a moment, knowing that Naito wanted deep information about their journey. Naito quickly bounced up and went to the pile of shiny tools in the corner of the hideout.

"We went into a human camp," Elite explained. "We were only after food but... I picked up this, uh... bag. I didn't realise what was in there."

Naito came bounding back to Elite on the opposite side of the bag with his teeth holding onto something small and pointy.

"Look. I got this," Naito said, spitting out the item into his paw. It was a bullet cartridge with some human inscription engraved on the side. Elite saw it and was reminded of the black magic product that he found after biting it inside the dead deer.

"So, I got it whilst paying the humans a visit. I had grown only a feathapaw in moons and... er..."

Naito's voice faded away and got Elite's attention. He had lowered his nose and relaxed his ears. The tail had stopped wagging too. Why did he just lose all his excitement like that?

"What is it, Naito?" he asked.

Hearing the golden male's concern had made Naito feel a bit safer. He lowered the bullet and returned Elite's glance with puppy eyes, looking full of regret.

"You see, growing up I used to have fascinations with humans and what they could bring to us. But no wolf in my family supported me for that. They stripped me of my name, Dusty. They even called me a coyote because I had made friends with humans."

"You were friends with them?" Elite asked, surprised.

"Well, not friends. Not really," admitted Naito. "But I was a familiar visitor. They used to give me gifts every day I could see them. Including this thing."

Elite could see the momentary smile from Naito as he recalled his memory. It seemed he enjoyed the company of humans, which was unheard of.

"That sounds... strange," Elite said cautiously.

"I was born in a bloodline kinship, you see. Los Vagabundos Desolados. Our group travelled North for generations to escape the human influence. After I was kicked out, I went insane for a while, running on my own. Didn't understand my purpose. But then... I found the Wise Wolf."

Elite's eyes widened. The Wise Wolf. He had met him too. The same wolf who almost killed his father... had met Naito as well? Elite lowered the weapon to look Naito in the eyes.

"He showed me what this object meant," Naito continued. "He says it's called a bullet. But the best part of all: he could read the writing on it."

The golden male's paws began to twitch. This was becoming rather awkward. Coincidental. Wulfur could also read the language of the humans. Why did the Wise Wolf have so much in common with his father?

Naito resumed his story, holding the bullet up to Elite. "This bullet says NATO on the end. I've been trying to figure out how that can be. But the Wise Wolf, he gave me guidance. After, he made Sapphina my kinswolf and sent us both to this pack."

He paused for a moment, rubbing the tip of the bullet against his chin. "Heh, funny that. Pack. We are more like an aspect, and I don't know why Alpha Oslo wants us to follow dated traditions. But still, no wolf cared about my discoveries, but I live to the Wise Wolf's words that someday... it will matter."

After Naito mentioned about pack tradition, Elite quickly shifted his attention back to the bullet.

"And that's how you uh... got your name?" he guessed, keeping his shoulders tight and legs close together.

Naito smiled again, raising his snout in a more friendly fashion. They were less than an apple's length away from touching noses. Naito could feel Elite's breath made cold by his lack of emotional response, whilst Elite shivered at the warm ambience from Naito's voice.

"Yeah. I gave it a ringy twist though. I have a lot of respect for humanity and would give much of my world to them. Oh, speaking of that. Come."

Naito led the way to his nest. Elite left the bag behind to follow him below the tree. They both were inside the hollowed area. It felt warm and secluded. Whilst Naito bent his head down to rummage beneath his nest, Elite narrowed his eyes, focusing on the serene ambience of the den. The sounds of croaking frogs quite distant, the trickling of the pondwater, the wavey grass beyond the tree roots and the dragonflies accumulating near the water surface. Elite felt oddly relaxed, and it wasn't soured at all with Naito wagging his tail up high directly in front of him.

"Here it is!" Naito called out.

Elite snapped out of his trance and reverted to his usual frowny face. Naito had turned to him with a light but fuzzy object in his left paw.

"They call this a dreamcatcher," he expounded. "The humans make them. Well, I made this. I wanted to give them this as a peace offering to show that wolves are nice and that we could work together!"

Elite took a long and careful look at the bizarre object. It had a strange netting material surrounded with stones, cobwebs, animal teeth and small vines. Naito placed the dreamcatcher to his side and began to slowly circle around Elite.

"Maybe if you ventured with us, you might get that chance," Elite jokingly rambled.

"I'd like that," Naito said in a more alluring tone behind where Elite was sitting. The golden male felt Naito's breath on the back of his neck. He turned his head left and right to see Naito walking with a slight imbalance on his legs. Elite stood up and showed his side in a defensive way, seeing Naito holding another unusual item in his jaws. It was sharp, made of stone and had a few vines holding it together. Elite was the wolf backed into the tree's hollow interior instead of Naito.

"Um... what are you doing?" Elite asked with his hackles raised. The tips of his claws pressed into the tender materials on Naito's nest.

Naito slowly crept toward Elite with his heart beating rapidly, like after an exhausting hunt. Elite found himself backpedalling a paw at a time, unsure of Naito's intentions.

"I really like you, Elite," the male scout replied through his clenched jaws, trying not to drop the sharp stone. "I feel blessed upon by the Greater Ones that I got to meet you."

Elite felt a combination of internal panic as his rear met the tree walls and his ears absorbing the title of the ancestors spoken by another that wasn't his father. Elite was sure that Naito had some trouble being a normal wolf but hearing that he still put faith in the divines, that Wulfur had accustomed Elite to avoiding, was both confusing and scary.

"Has any wolf told you that before?" asked Naito. He let his pupils drift over the golden male, feeling more and more eager to be close with him.

"No," Elite winced, feeling his tail rub against the thick wood. "No wolf dare say such blasphemy to me." His voice was hasty, and his ears were flattened to the sides.

"Oh. I am surprised. How could any wolf ignore your gorgeous golden fur?" Naito continued to near up to Elite. The golden male found himself sinking submissively below the happy wolf. Naito's tail wagged rapidly. He gave Elite a trance-like stare.

Elite didn't know what to do. Should he tell him to back off? Should he just run out without saying anything? No, that couldn't happen. He needed to keep Naito busy. By staying and enduring these feelings, his father Wulfur would surely find enough time to raid the prey pile. Elite now had his back laid against the tree, the tall Naito casting a shadow completely over him. Elite closed his eyes and held his breath.

When Elite had a few seconds to realise he wasn't feeling any pain, he opened his eyes to the sound of a thud, like a rock dropping from a cliff edge. He peered down his own chest to see that Naito had crawled between his legs and had his brisket close to Elite's belly. But the sharp stone was no longer in Naito's mouth. It had been cast off into the dirt behind Naito's tail and he now had his jaws free. The golden male spoke with a tone of puppy-like fear.

"Oh, you aren't going to hurt me?" Elite said with a wobble in his speech.

"What?" Naito tilted his head in disbelief. "Why would I do that?"

Elite didn't want to assume anything. He hated being wrong. He wasn't sure how to tell Naito that no wolf had come this close without physically hurting him, besides his father most of the time.

"I get into... a lot of fights with other wolves," Elite said, deciding to keep as vague as possible. Naito looked at Elite's tucked forelegs, seeing some of the scars from his fight with Wulfur.

"What, like those? They look fresh," Naito commented as he raised his stomach to see past down to Elite's hind legs, noticing more scars on his hocks and paws. "What happened to you?"

"Nothing. Don't worry about it," Elite said, turning his head away from Naito and closing his eyes, shutting out any interest in the discussion.

"Oh, come on, handsome," Naito wooed. "If a colony of squirrels dropped you from their tree and you landed in a crocodile-infested swamp, then I get why you'd keep quiet, haha. You can tell me, no other wolf's going to know."

He reached a paw to stroke Elite on the cheek after saying that. Elite twitched before opening his eyes. Naito's touch was calming and energising at the same time. With a chilled sigh, Elite opened up to him.

"It was my father. I said some things that made him angry, and I tried to eat his food."

At this point, Elite had the energy and courage to raise his head again, taking in the radiance of Naito's body which was nearly resting on top of him.

"Fathers are like that," Naito explained. "They're sometimes jealous of how special you are."

Elite never thought about that. Could his father be jealous of his abilities and quick wits? Elite was now staring directly at Naito's endearing face, his eyes full of life and ears steaming hot.

"I know you're special..." Naito whispered in Elite's ear. "...and I am going to show you how much I know so."

A small portion of Elite's internal panic tried to arise, looking to neutralise the situation.

"B-but... but the prey pile. You should b-b-be guarding it and the... your Alpha. He might get mad at you and..."

Elite's arrogant complaints were finally silenced by the weight of Naito resting firmly over his body. Their noses almost brushed together when Elite lowered his snout after feeling Naito's warm breath invade his nostrils. Elite could now see inside Naito's mouth. His fangs, how they looked when they weren't ripping into flesh. So clean and strong, unlike his tongue that appeared soft, spongy and oddly enticing. It withered with Naito's breath, causing Elite to let out a lustrous gasp for air.

"Ohhh, Naito," Elite whispered in a tone of acceptance and surrender to the embrace proposed from the wolf on top of him. "Your teeth, they are... mildly inviting."

Naito gave a snarky smile and then went for a light lick on Elite's nose tip. The golden male didn't react negatively.

"You want a little taste?" Naito teased to Elite.

The young male didn't answer. He gently lifted his head and exposed his teeth and tongue in alluring obedience. Naito slowly opened his jaws too, much wider, allowing Elite to navigate his snout between Naito's lips. Naito let his upper weight drop on Elite, letting the playful and excitable energy take over.

They both closed their eyes during their intimate exchange of saliva, knowing they both wanted it. Elite felt the tenseness in his shoulders vanish as Naito used his paws to grip the ground, feeling himself lose balance and almost fall off the other wolf. Both their tails wagged in harmony. Naito positioned himself in a way that brought most of his belly and limbs into contact with the other. He confidently caressed Elite's fur, whilst Elite slowly gave in to the temptation to stroke him back.

The hideout was hot, and full of radiance. The pair casted a singular shadow against the tree as the setting sun peeked through its' roots. With the sound of fur rustling and tongues popping, they joined in with the natural ambience of the nearby lake.

Chapter 10

Wulfur looked to his left. The entrance was unguarded, and it was getting too dark to see the exterior. It could be the best option for their immediate escape, but he would need to grab Elite first. Hopefully what was left of his special herbal remedy would be enough to make all the wolves nearby turn drowsy. Then he fully checked the remainder of his surroundings. Finally, it had gone quiet. Zavi and Fenn were asleep a couple of yards away from him. The pups were still cosied up around Leyla and the occasional chatter could barely be heard from under the tree. Sounds like Elite had done his job.

He stood up and bit into a leaf from the pile he had laid on. Dragging it quietly to the centre of the clearing, Wulfur kept his eyes on the pair of hunters in case they twitched an ear at him. With the leaf in place, Wulfur then fiddled with the herbs, trying to get as much as he could at once into a paw. With each careful transportation, Wulfur brought traces of lavender, blue lotus, chamomile and valerian root to the leaf. Each of his footsteps were carefully placed, avoiding the tiniest of twigs. A single snap could put the whole plan into jeopardy.

With all the herbs gathered, the old timber male returned to the lone duffel bag and opened his jaws, getting a grip on the water container. It then slipped from his mouth, the glass grinding against his teeth, making an ear-tightening scratch. The bottle landed back in the bag, bopping itself on the matchbox. Wulfur poised for an attack, seemingly sure they would have heard that. Nothing. No wolf noticed the odd sound. No ears had perked up. Wulfur sighed in relief.

He took a gulp of air before trying again. This time, he would hold a paw against the container to make sure it couldn't leave his mouth. He limped over and placed the item on its side. Wulfur saw it start to roll away, causing him to catch it in a hurry. He felt a bit annoyed by the complexity of these human trinkets. At least he didn't need to go to the river for water, let alone find a way to carry so much of it.

Last, but not least, Wulfur moved the matchbox up toward his artistic creation. It all looked like a display of favourite things. But Wulfur knew it was about to become a nightmare. *'I hope this works just like I saw before,'* he thought, heading back to the bag. *'And that the little runt left me enough to affect all the wolves here.'* He softly grunted, once again reminded of how much more flawless this plan could have been if it weren't for Elite's daft act.

He went for the deer hide scrap at the bottom of the bag and coaxed it over his nose. Using his paws, he repositioned it to shield his nostrils and lips from fresh air whilst padding it to make it more comfortable. This was it for Wulfur. He had to put his plan into action now.

When he got back to his little assembly of herbs, he sat down and used his claw to carefully open the matchbox. Knowing that he would accidentally set the deer hide on fire, Wulfur was forced to use his claws instead of his teeth to hold the match. After wedging the clean end of the stick between his digits, the male struck the darker end against the side of the box, which he held still with the other paw. The match ignited, Wulfur almost flinching at the magical light. Its little flame settled, reflecting a burning soul into Wulfur's eyes. He remembered that time was not on his side, so he threw the match into the herb pile.

As expected, the fire began to spread. However, Wulfur soon realised that the surrounding grass had also caught fire. He stood up and backed away from the flames, nearly knocking over the water container. It budged, shaking the liquid inside. Wulfur knew he needed to act quickly.

Feeling for a gap beneath the makeshift mask, he bit the lid of the container, popped it off, and clumsily barged it into the flames. The leaf pile was extinguished, now releasing an eerie dark smoke into the air. It rapidly spread around the clearing. Wulfur found himself distracted by the remaining flames as they continued to spread. There were only a few inches of it, but there was no more water to stop it, nor the time to worry.

Wulfur headed back to the bag, leaving the container and matchbox behind. He fed his head under the strap, hoisting it up and over his neck, then made a light jog toward the prey pile. A dark smile soon appeared under his mask; part of his teeth could be seen glowing from the ambience of the fire. Yet, the deer pelt was doing a good job of making sure he didn't inhale the fumes. He didn't want to end up like Elite the other day. Drowsy and weak. He knew that soon all the wolves in the pack would be in a trance.

On approach to the prey pile, Wulfur checked his corners. No sign of Naito, nor any wolf for that matter. His adrenaline kicked in as his eyes focused in on the remaining food stash. *'The pack might be a bit odd, but they sure knew how to hunt well,'* he thought. *'Time to take everything they got!'*

He lowered the bag right in front of the protein-rich scraps and began scooping meat. Each covered bone and stripped flesh piece reddened his paws, the smell of prey breaching past his mask. This fuelled Wulfur to scramble for larger chunks faster. His breathing became heavy and so did the bag. Only for a moment did he shiver at the thought of his own insanity being caused by the smoky mess he left in the clearing. He would have been dead meat himself if he passed out now.

Itch aside, he neared to a full bag of food with the prey pile reduced to pointy bone-ends and fur strands. Then he heard a twig snap. A rather deliberate sound. Wulfur froze for a second before whipping his whole body around to see where it had come from. A dark grey wolf stood there with a formal pose. But they also had some kind of animal skin over their nose.

"So, you really thought that infiltrating my pack and taking my food was going to be this easy?" asked the approaching wolf.

That question made it clear who this was, along with the distinct voice. Wulfur arched his back, defending the bag of food behind his legs.

"Well, I made it this far, Oslo," Wulfur sneered. "Your leadership is clearly terrible. Now I'm going to make you pay for it."

Alpha Oslo chuckled darkly beneath the mask, protecting him from the smoke. He made small steps toward Wulfur, trying to evoke some kind of power over him.

"I can assure you, Wulfur, this was all part of the plan," the Alpha said, stiffening his shoulders.

"What plan?" Wulfur said angrily, once again conflicting bewilderment and achievement of this Alpha knowing his real name without needing to tell him. "The Wise Wolf told you my name, didn't he? If you knew to cover your nose, why didn't you do the same for the others? Why aren't your hunters up here now fighting with you? You actually think you can take me down by yourself? You're weak and pathetic!"

Oslo stopped advancing and raised his head, making his sharp teeth visible to Wulfur. His voice held calm, yet convincing.

"The Wise Wolf assured me this would work and well, here we are. Why don't you surrender now? Let us turn you in, in exchange for your life. Justice gets served, and so will my reward."

Wulfur stamped his foot into the ground. He would not tolerate this Alpha's gentle approach any longer.

"CHOKE ON A BONE!" the timber male growled. "The rewards are lies! You're a pawn to that cave dweller!" His eyes showed his internal rage from the light behind Oslo. This made him look back at the fire. It was flashier than before and boasted an orange ambience throughout the den.

"Alpha Oslo, where are you?" whimpered a weary, light female voice from the clearing. A voice that Wulfur hadn't heard before. "Help! There's fire, I think. I don't know, I can't see properly!"

Oslo turned his head in the direction of his Alpha rock and his ears dropped.

"Freya!" he cried.

In that immediate instant, Wulfur charged at Oslo and knocked him onto the grass, spine first. Their dramatic leap together through the air was enough to slide the animal skin off Oslo's face. Knowing he'd have no time to put it back on, he began trying to bite Wulfur's neck.

Wulfur towered over him, scratching at Oslo's brisket each time he raised his head. Oslo kept missing his lunges and was already fatiguing out, partly because of the calming scent in the air affecting the others. His vision became poorer and poorer, losing sense and thought of his potentially endangered packmates.

"Like I said..." Wulfur taunted between tactical defences. "Weak."

"You know who else is weak?" Oslo chanted, the serenity of the smoke already getting to his head. Wulfur held him still so that he could talk, but tight enough so that he couldn't break free. "Your boy. Naito should have finished him by now. All part of the plan, hehehe."

Wulfur's eyes widened over the upper part of his protective gear. Then he pounded at Oslo's neck with both paws, making the Alpha gag and spit blood.

"You've been planning to let that dusty boy kill my son?!" Wulfur's voice was no longer muffled by the mask as it hanged on end whilst his nose was aimed downward. "THAT'S IT! I'LL KILL YOU!"

Wulfur bounced off the Alpha and stood by the prey pile guard point and waited for him to get up. Oslo took to each of his own legs, slipping each paw trying to grip the dirt. His head was spinning and Wulfur became a blur in his sights. He let out a yawn which he did not expect after eventually rising.

He saw the timber blur enlarge before feeling his chest get rammed by Wulfur's head. They both carried momentum toward the prey pile. Wulfur repelled the Alpha's body away after he stopped charging. Oslo crashed into the mess of bones, feeling a few impale his back. The carcass bones were tough enough to suspend him off the ground. Oslo felt almost nothing as even sounds around him began to fuzz. The last normal thing he could think about was how such an aroma existed, and how a wolf could ever feel this way.

It was done, but Oslo was still breathing. Wulfur approached and pondered about how he would finish him. But then he thought for a moment about his reputation. If the Alpha was dead, there would be no wolf to tell of his story. To tell others that Wulfur was a fearsome wolf. He looked into the eyes of the fallen Alpha and let out an evil scoff.

"Taking advice from a lonely cave dweller. Challenging me on your own. The Wise Wolf played you. Now you're going to suffer the consequences. Not so much the happy bunch anymore, are we?" Wulfur stood proudly, enjoying watching the Alpha grimace over his defeat and pack mockery.

Amongst the wincing and unavoidable scent from the herbal smoke, Oslo had enough sanity to talk back to the dominant timber wolf.

"The Wise Wolf is more dangerous than you know. He helped form my pack, at the cost of the ancestral advancement. Many wolves died in his name." Oslo wriggled and wrestled with no prevail from the deepening wounds. His paws flailed spontaneously as he experienced painless bliss at the mercy of the aromatic black cloud.

"Sounds like he wanted to destroy you too," Wulfur replied, his eyes glowing from the now enraged flames in the clearing. The sounds of panicked wolves behind them became louder and more desperate. "Guess he knew I'd overthrow you. How... humbling." On that last remark, Wulfur hoisted the bag of food over his shoulder and left Oslo to deal with his spinning head and punctured muscles.

Oslo was too weak to dislodge himself from the bones underneath him. He twitched and struggled, but he could not fight it. Not anymore. "Oh, Greater Ones, what have I done? I plead for your aid," he chanted in a whisper, his blood-drowned throat made it hard to be heard.

Wulfur dashed through the clearing around its edge. The fire was stunning when he went up this close. It had spread to the Alpha's rock, the trainees' den and the nursery grounds. He could feel death amongst the heat. Wulfur realised what had happened when he looked back at his leaf pile. The matchbox was in little bits, barely anything left besides crisp debris that continued to deteriorate in the epicentre of flames. All the other matches must have been set off too. Zavi and Fenn were no longer next to the source.

Wherever they went, Wulfur knew there was no time to find out. He needed to save Elite or kill Naito if it was too late. Or both. Wulfur liked that idea. He rushed toward the giant tree and slid down the narrow pathway.

Meanwhile, under the tree, the pair of wolves had switched places and were interlocked with their hind legs. Elite was resting his weight on top of Naito, still alive and breathing, whilst Naito was holding him tightly against his body, his left front paw on Elite's neck scruff and the other pressing on the base of his tail. On the front end, they had both their eyes shut, taking careful and caring analysis of each other's breath. The sound and smell partially blinded them from the ruckus outside.

"What's that commotion?" Elite said softly, hearing a few distant cries and picking up the tiniest hint of burning essence.

Naito simply smiled, squinting his eyes open slightly and letting his paw slide past and almost under Elite's tail.

"There's no other wolf here, what commotion?" he taunted playfully.

Elite felt Naito's touch and it made him tingle, enough to pull his head up and take notice of the light-yellow glow coming from the entrance. Along with it, a large and fast-moving shadow, accompanied by rapid paw stomps, getting louder and louder.

"Elite!" the shadow called out.

The familiar guttural voice made Elite move his paws behind Naito's head and forced his chest up, breaking free from the top half of Naito's intimate leg trap.

"Father?" Elite responded, his tail dropping like a dead flower.

They both looked over to see Wulfur violently charge toward them with his bag of food swaying everywhere. Elite saw the bizarre mask over his face and couldn't remember what it was for. Wulfur slowed when he got near and gave Elite a firm but painless shove off Naito, breaking the warmth they had under their flanks.

"What are you doing?!" Elite complained, grunting from the force of his father's head into his ribs.

Once Elite was tossed aside, Wulfur aligned himself with Naito, growling aggressively.

"You! Trying to kill Elite! You're finished! Just like your Alpha!" he barked under the animal skin covering his nose.

Naito flailed his legs, trying to stand upright again. He had been so comforted and so aroused by Elite that his exposure like this in a fight was rather embarrassing. But to top it all off, the father of his love interest caught them in the act. After a few moments of confusion, Naito found his way to his feet. He felt his own rump aching from being pressed against the ground by his new golden partner.

Both Elite and Naito attempted to stop Wulfur with panicked words and pleading gestures.

"Woah, woah, woah, hey! I'm not trying to kill him," said Naito, holding his paw up in a pathetic attempt to block a potential lunge.

"Father, Naito's fine! He didn't hurt me," said Elite, nearly standing in Wulfur's way, not ashamed with the lustful state of his body.

"I heard what your Alpha said, dusty boy!" Wulfur explained, removing the mask, realising that the lower ground meant that his special scent didn't get under the tree. He exposed his deadly teeth and snapped at the coffee-pelted scout. "You were meant to kill him down here! What's that there? A weapon?"

Wulfur pointed with his nose at the discarded sharp stone left close to where they laid. Naito looked at it, then back toward Wulfur.

"Hold up, muscle wolf. This is a misunderstanding!" Naito expressed contemptuously, edging away from the hollow tree. "I was-...*we* were having just a little bit of... aldrstenal courtship?"

Naito smiled awkwardly at Wulfur, who looked less pleased with that response. A courtship was a courtship, no way around that for Naito. Wulfur knew of the word 'aldrsten' in the ancient folktales. It meant 'to be male', so it could be applied to anything that male wolves did, together or not. Wulfur found this concept to be riveting, yet highly disturbing. His face grumbled, painting a picture in his head of what kind of 'courting' Naito had drawn Elite into.

"What's going on?" Elite asked his father.

Wulfur felt partially relieved to have his mind pulled away from their little romance game. But Elite stood in Wulfur's way, striking a defensive pose.

"Why are you down here?" Elite continued to question. "You done? Already?"

Wulfur sighed heavily, knowing that killing Naito would sour their trust. Maybe he should have seen this coming. Elite was protecting another wolf of the same sex. A wolf he was interested in. Good and proper. At least there wouldn't be any accidental litters. But there was no way this 'Naito' was going to stay forever. Naito knew how to kill wolves with foreign objects. He would have to get rid of him later.

"Yes, I got the food. The den, it's burning down," said Wulfur.

"What?!" Naito exclaimed, his eyes growing wide with surprise.

"Shut it, you!" Wulfur snapped before looking back up the path toward the fire. "We need to get out, but the way back up is too dangerous. We won't be able to breathe."

Wulfur looked around Naito's hideout, slightly bewildered by all the small trinkets and fabrics the young male had collected. It wasn't looking good. Besides straight into the water beneath the tree roots, there was no hiding let alone escaping.

"Are we trapped?" Elite asked.

"Not exactly," Naito broke in before Wulfur could moan some more. His voice was snarky again but showed a bit of hollowness. Such an expression was hard to maintain when he was thinking about the horrible things his pack might be experiencing up above.

The old father turned slowly to Naito who was cautiously creeping away from the inside of the tree.

"What do you mean? You have another way out, dusty boy? Tell me!" Wulfur demanded.

"Father, calm down," Elite pleaded, raising his head. His nose almost reached the height of Wulfur's. "And his name's Naito, not Dusty."

For a moment, Naito couldn't speak. He was admiring Elite's bravery. The golden male had stepped in for him. This big brute of a father getting challenged by his son. Impressive. It only made him like Elite more. Maybe their close interaction did something for Elite. Either way, Naito calmed and regained some enthusiasm to his voice.

"I do. But we may get a little wet. If you spare me, I shall lead the way."

Wulfur was reluctant to agree with this. What if it was another trap? Given that Naito was pointing at the water beneath the tree, it couldn't possibly be back towards the pack. The timber male observed the drop.

Elite exhaled aggressively through his nose, letting his breath touch Wulfur's face. He then went to pack the bag with the stuff he had shared to Naito. He felt good about that moment. Standing up to his father didn't feel so hard when it was Naito he was protecting. But now that his father was here to stay, Elite's frown reformed. But he kept his head above his shoulders, unlike times before where he would cower below.

"Fine, Naito," Wulfur growled, withdrawing his eye contact from him. "But if you put a paw wrong, it'll be your neck."

Naito had no idea what Wulfur's problem was. The unfatherly attitude Wulfur had toward Elite made him angry in his core. The knowledge that Elite's scars were caused by this psycho of a father only amplified his dismay.

Regrettably, Naito nodded with a foul smirk and moved out from under the tree, creeping up to Elite. When the golden male lifted his head from the duffel bag, he was greeted by a loving lick to his cheek. Naito beamed at him.

"I know this is my pack, but they don't see my vision..." Naito picked up his dreamcatcher from the side and plopped it into the bag. "But you do, Elite. So, I'm going with you."

At first, Elite wasn't sure of the idea of a third wolf in their group. But this was Naito, the wolf that heightened his interest and made Elite feel things he didn't know he could feel. It felt right and Elite had to believe it. It only depended on Wulfur's lenience that Naito could come along.

He put on an uncharacteristic smile toward Naito. Their eyes were connected like two carefully tied rope-ends. Naito had such a charming stare that Elite couldn't resist. Naito's face represented his snarky voice, all the fur that Elite touched, and those teeth. Those inviting teeth. Elite huffed in delight and Naito did the same.

Wulfur watched the pair very closely before moving himself nearer to the thick tree roots.

"Come on! We don't have time for this!" he barked at them.

Naito slowly turned his head and gave another nod to Wulfur, this time more sarcastically. When he looked back, Elite had mounted the bag over his neck and had shaken it over his shoulder.

"It's so cool how you can carry them like that," Naito remarked. "Okay, down here."

Naito bounced toward where Wulfur stood, leaving him a bit of distance. He then leapt down between the third and fourth root from the left and splashed into the shallow pondwater. Elite chased him down, to then be followed by Wulfur. Naito was unable to turn around through this narrow route, but he kept talking whilst looking ahead.

"Jeeva used to say *'oh, no Naito, you can't go through here, it's all muddy and mushy and I'm thin and still can't get through'*..." Naito rambled from up front. His ears picked up the sounds of multiple paws treading behind him, so he knew they were following closely. "...In fact, all the wolves think they can't cut through the forest from den side. But I did a bit of work with my human stuff and proved them wrong."

Naito let his mind wander as he crept through the overgrowth of weeds. Elite observed the atmosphere of this route, noticing how the plants could hold back the rain from under here. His hocks were cold under the water, but it didn't seem to bother him that much. He also had a nice view of Naito's tail, giving off a musky scent that kept him encouraged to stay close.

Wulfur behind was having thoughts about their next move. So, he had learned from the pack of unquiet dreams that the Wise Wolf was a manipulator. He played Alpha Oslo by gaining his trust through success of the pack and the downfall of others. Wulfur was curious to know what other aspects and kinships fell during the ancestral advancement. He was sure those events happened a few years ago, toward the East of this land.

He felt the bag of food scrape the walls of the tunnel, causing him to grunt. Elite was smaller and more agile than him, and he was able to carve through the vegetation much faster. He almost lost sight of his son's golden tail as they reached the dry land. Their paws were muddy, and their fur pelts took a lot of chlorophyll off the tickly weeds. The path finally started to open, and each wolf shook themselves to eliminate that claustrophobic sensation. Naito would shake the fastest, being the only wolf without carry weight.

"We did it. We're out," Naito announced. But as he turned around to look back at the escape route, his attention was diverted to above the trees, where he could see the cloud of smoke and glow of orange. The glow was fire, burning what he had left behind. For a moment, he went quiet. He stared blankly up at whatever stars he could still see when Elite approached him.

"Naito, are you okay?" Elite asked, his voice more concerned for another than ever before.

"You…" Naito responded softly. "…you both are the Goldfire. The Wise Wolf spoke the truth."

Elite tilted his head, trying to understand Naito's thought process about loss. It was not familiar to Elite, so he paid attention to Naito's reactions.

Wulfur emerged, hearing the last part of Naito's verdict. He breathed heavily, feeling strain from the long time spent crouched behind the pair.

"And he won't be speaking much more. I am going… we… we are going to kill him."

The area went quiet, only the raging flames in the distance murmured over their breaths. Wulfur looked around, using his nose to get his bearings. He had been here before. This was close to the place where he and Elite met the crazy jester wolf.

"Even mentor Quade didn't know about this shortcut. And he's very smart," Naito commented with a slight grin. He thought he regained his confidence, but then he realised the dire truth of tonight and sighed regretfully. "But he's probably dead now."

Elite sat next to Naito where he stood and leaned his neck away from him. Naito instantly placed his chin on Elite's shoulder, seeking comfort in a place that wasn't home. Naito didn't whimper about it, but deep down he knew that he'd have to start over. With Elite. Wulfur was a stick in the dirt to their relationship, but it didn't bother him that much. Wulfur advanced toward the gap in the forest that they'd followed before the bear encounter and waited for Elite and Naito.

"Let's go before any survivors track us down," said Wulfur commandingly.

He watched his son comfort Naito. This was a problem. He knew Naito would make Elite weak. Wulfur needed Elite to be strong and this new companion was a step in the wrong direction. Somehow, somewhere, Naito had to go.

Chapter 11

It was the middle of the night. Crickets in the woods chirped without end, and owls tooted their eerie melodies from their nests in the shrouded trees. Wulfur led the way through the darkness, with Elite and Naito taking a slow trudge behind him. The coffee-pelted wolf took an occasional glance at the bags Elite and Wulfur were carrying.

"The humans are so clever. Why didn't we think of carrying prey like that? But I suppose even if we knew we could, I'm not sure how we'd make them in the first place!" Naito spoke with more energy now he was once again in a comfortable place at Elite's side.

Ahead, Wulfur rolled his eyes. Naito was too enthusiastic for his liking. The older male kept his pace, gaining distance over the pair of lovebirds.

Elite turned his head to see the bag over his own shoulder, then huffed confidently back at Naito. "You said you could read the human writing? Why not ask them to tell you?" Elite questioned him.

"No, silly, not me. I'd have to ask the Wise Wolf to decipher it," Naito replied.

"Or my father," Elite said, dropping his head low, eyes remaining focused ahead. "He can read human writing too, can't you father?" He hoped to spike his father's involvement in the conversation. Elite heard a light but deep huff from Wulfur. Nothing else though.

"Really? He can? Oh..." Naito thought for a moment, his eyes wandering loosely as if he were in a daydream. "That's odd, the Wise Wolf told me he could read because the Greater Ones blessed him with the power."

"Yeah, that *is* odd..." Elite agreed, still staring ahead, seeing Wulfur with his ears alert and slowing movement. His words slowed with suspicion. "That's also my fathers' explanation."

Naito let out a light hum, accompanied by a smile. "Maybe they're related. Maybe *you're* related."

"Blasphemy," Elite said with a light chuckle, which was uncharacteristic for him over such a crazy suggestion. "I've tried to understand my own name that appears on this carry-um, I mean bag. I just don't get how it works."

For a few seconds, the pair looked around the forest, thinking of a new ice breaker to their discussion. Then Elite turned his head to Naito once more with sincere interest.

"Naito, who are the Greater Ones?"

Up ahead, Wulfur's fur raised on his spine. The smell of a swamp soon invaded his nostrils. The grounds where Elite and Wulfur had their fight were nearby. Naito could say what he wanted, but Wulfur was certain, in the direction he was heading, it would all be for nothing.

Naito pondered over Elite's question as they strolled between some closely packed trees, Elite almost having to step through first to avoid them both getting stuck. But the golden male would prefer that happened instead of keeping up with his careless father.

"You don't know?" Naito asked.

"Well, sort of," Elite quietly admitted. "I only learned they were a thing last moon."

Naito then glanced at Elite's father. *'Why did Wulfur not teach Elite about the ancestors?'* he thought. He spoke softly toward Elite.

"Well, they are the coupapaw of wolf gods that gave us freedom to roam the lands," Naito explained.

This was only the beginning of the truths Elite wanted to uncover. Unlike his ignorant self, the golden male took to his heart everything Naito was justifying. All the things he had suspected from the pack he'd escaped from before encountering the Wise Wolf. And all the wolves seemed to know about these divine spirits, no matter what aspect they came from. He continued to listen to Naito.

"You tried howling at the full moon before? Those whispers, that's them responding to us."

"Uh, no. No, I haven't," said Elite.

Naito lowered his ears, a low grumble came from his throat and his smile disappeared faster than a rabbit down a burrow.

"Oh, Elite. You should. They'd give you guidance."

"I don't think so." Elite gestured his refusal of belief by wavering his paw. "What were their names?"

"The Greater Ones?" Naito asked, perking up again. "Easy! Liko, Blade, Raven and Ulfur. That last 'One' sounds a lot like your father, haha."

"Yeah, I know. That was the only 'One' he ever told me about." Elite felt embarrassed. He felt like his father raised him up to only be dumbfounded by other wolves and therefore rejected in their society. This made sense and gave Elite an assumption of what it meant to be a loner. No friends? A detachment from reality? Denial of the primary divinity? Elite curved his claws tensely, forcing them to dig into the dirt with each step.

"Sounds like there's a lot for me to teach you," Naito said with a spring in his stride, nearly bouncing his way ahead of Elite. Just then, Elite stopped. His eyes were darting in different directions, but his nose kept aim at the ground.

Yes, he wanted to know what parts of wolf culture he missed growing up. But he had been accustomed to his fathers' ways for so long that he conflicted the idea of just throwing it all aside for a new outlook. He remembered the ancestral spirit gate symbols from last moon. The symbols Wulfur had trained him to avoid. Wulfur had made him fearful of it. Turns out understanding the Greater Ones for what they were truly worth to wolfkind was going to be painful.

"I... I can't. You can't teach me," Elite said with a stumble in his speech. "I'm too scared to know the truth. I am comfortable with what I know. I don't want to confront the spirits."

Naito watched Elite lower his head, almost cowering where he stood.

The former scout gently approached, expression friendly and tone inviting.

"You got me, Elite. If you love me, I'm sure you'd be willing to let me try."

Love? Is that what Elite had felt when they were cuddling? Wulfur did say love felt good. Elite had a brainwave that maybe if Naito kept him feeling this way, he'd be able to bypass his fear of the Greater Ones' true purpose.

Elite slowly stepped forward, face-to-face with his newfound partner, Naito's excitement proudly displayed from his supersonic tail-wagging. They gently rubbed noses, followed by Naito sending a quick lick past Elite's snout, just stopping beneath his eye. The golden wolf again cracked a smile, which wouldn't likely be his reaction to any other wolf.

"I do love you, Naito. Thanks," said Elite.

"I love you too, Elite," Naito cooed back. "And I know I can help you."

They both closed their eyes for a moment, sensing each other's presence. Elite had a conflicting feeling in his body. The tingle of lust for Naito was crawling through his fur whilst his inner arrogance and denial for truth tried to fight it away. For Naito, he felt like he had found his future. He was ready to put aside his past and act as a guide for Elite, though still unsure of what Wulfur would do to sour that ambition.

That then led to another thought. What of the Wise Wolf? Naito couldn't believe that Wulfur was serious about killing the wolf who guided him to sanity and gave him a reason to join Alpha Oslo's pack. *'That could wait'*, he thought. Now was the time to bond with Elite. Get to know him more. Spend days and nights together. He let out a giggle before turning and getting back onto the scent trail after Wulfur. Elite, feeling smitten by the lick, wagged his tail lightly and went to follow Naito, eager to keep up with him.

They quietly moved through the darkness, occasionally grazing on each other's pelts. Elite had a lot of fun speaking with Naito, but in very little time, he soon realised that his father hadn't explained exactly how they were going to kill The Wise Wolf. Normally he'd have a plan up front. Wulfur wasn't in their sights. Elite could smell him ahead but still wanted that sense of assurance that he was safe. Did Naito not make him feel safe?

"Father?" Elite called out ahead of him. No response. After a few more steps into an open area, Elite suddenly remembered where they were. The fog, the loud crickets, the eerie green murk in the air that smelt of frothy dirt. The golden male stopped, hoping for his fathers' reply amongst the shadows.

"Perhaps we scared him off," Naito joked. The coffee-pelted male looked around the clearing. Then back at Elite. "We should move faster."

The air felt heavy, and the other woodland creatures had stopped contributing to the ambience. Elite looked around curiously for his father whilst Naito took in the nearby scents. He squinted his eyes in a particular direction, smelling something different. And hostile.

Suddenly, a deep, loud growl could be heard to their left. Deeper than any wolf could imitate. Elite matched his sensory direction with Naito to spot a lone bear rotating its neck aggressively and advancing forward at them.

"A bear! Naito, run!" Elite shouted. He scampered in the opposite direction but found himself stopping when he noticed that Naito hadn't moved.

"What? Run? Don't be silly, Elite. We can take it on!" Naito stood firmly, opposing the massive furry figure with a challenging grin.

"But my father said that a paw of wolves can't fight a bear," argued Elite with a panicked face.

"Well, then where is he? Your father?" Naito posed himself for an attack on the bear, rooting for Elite to join him on the intimidation game. "Make us a paw and talon against this fat chunk."

"Over here." The familiar rough voice came from the direction Elite nearly ran in.

"Father!" Elite bellowed. The timber-pelted brute stood amongst the fog, his silhouette perfectly placed between the trees, like he was the guardian of an ominous gateway. Elite looked up the crest and gave his father a nervous order. "Help us, will you?!"

Wulfur didn't come forward. The bear was nearing and there wasn't much time before they'd clash.

"Up the tree, Elite," Wulfur commanded. Elite began to feel flustered, looking back at his father for guidance. Was he serious? There was now enough of them to fight the bear, and he still insisted on using their trained evasion tactic. A few seconds passed and Wulfur began to get aggressive.

"Elite, up the tree, now!" Wulfur's head nudged at the tree on his right. "Quickly!"

Elite looked back at Naito. He hadn't turned around. Instead, Naito had been fixated on the bear approaching slowly. His ears rotated, hearing Elite speak to him.

"Naito, can you climb a tree?"

This time, Naito briefly turned his head. He was a bit confused by this question.

"No, I can't," Naito replied. "But why? Let's just fight the bear. Come on."

"Don't listen to him, Elite!" Wulfur shouted back, stamping his foot into the ground. "Do as I say or you're both going to die!"

Elite was struggling to decide who to stick with. Naito, or the tree. Yes, it meant his own life would be saved. Or at least he could test how effective the height advantage was against a real threat. On the other paw, his newfound partner had no option but to run.

"What about Naito?" Elite asked. He frantically looked around for other options.

"He can come with me," replied Wulfur through gritted teeth. "Get up the tree and distract the bear. I'll get us to safety. Now!"

Elite twisted his body to make sure Naito was listening. They did not have time to debate.

"Naito, follow my father," Elite said desperately. "I'll be fine."

Naito let his eyes wander around the sight of the bear, who had closed right up into the clearing. It was brown, with a big black nose, claws the size of thick twigs and a jaw capable of engulfing a wolf's head. But Naito knew they could all gang up on this bear, and with enough coordination, kill it without any wolf seriously hurt. He sighed in disappointment before swiftly turning to Wulfur, watching Elite run at the tree.

Elite used all his training to get up the trunk, his front claws digging in all the right places to maintain grip. Despite the carry weight, his momentum got him up there rather fast, with his front paws making synchronised shifts in altitude and the rears acting as anchors. The profile of this tree was especially strong, allowing for Elite to mount himself onto a branch and only have his tail dangling below. The bear had just reached the middle of the clearing.

"Hey! Up here, clod-foot! My, my, you are ugly!" Elite taunted, waving his rump at the beast from below. The bear grunted as it jolted its head upward. It approached the tree and got its front paws up, pounding them against the massive base. The tree didn't budge, but the bear kept trying. Even a small leap to try and bite Elite's teasing tail.

Naito briefly looked back to see the distraction strategy from Elite. As amusing as it was to see it working, he still didn't favour this plan. Naito approached Wulfur with a frown as the old timber male turned and walked away.

Naito quietly followed Wulfur a few dozen metres down the crest and around the bank of a swamp, hearing the bear continue to make a ruckus from behind them. They both were out of sight and right near the mushy water when Wulfur came to a stop. Naito arrived with much adrenaline and gave Wulfur a look of dismay. He wasn't going to hide his distaste for Wulfur any longer.

"What sort of idea was that, you old grunter?" Naito questioned. He remained stood on his paws, wearingly watching Wulfur remove the duffel bag from his shoulder and circle him slowly until the swamp was directly behind him.

"All wolves know a paw and talon in wolves could defeat a lone bear. Don't tell me you're afraid of them and you made Elite feel the same. You can't let him grow up like thi-"

Like a snap of a twig, Wulfur raged and lunged at Naito, his jaw impaling Naito's chest. Naito grunted, feeling his body get slammed and sent charging backwards away from the lineup of formidable forest trees. The pair pirouetted off the narrow bank and into the water with a slimy splash.

Meanwhile, up the tree, Elite had stopped using his rear end as bait. The bear was patrolling around the trunk, looking for a way to get him down.

"Give up yet, fatback?" he mocked at the bear, not even smiling at his own power of offense. The bear returned Elite's questions with angry huffing noises through its' nose. Elite knew the arrogant energy he gave off was useful at annoying others, but he also knew who he was doing this for and that made him feel unsatisfied. The golden male stood on his fours on the impressively thick tree branch. The dense coverage of leaves made it hard for him to see anything but the bear.

"Elite! Jump down when he looks at me!" The voice was Wulfur, but Elite couldn't see him. The bear looked away from the tree to hear where Wulfur was barking from. Elite didn't hesitate to ready himself for a jump.

The golden wolf swooped down like an eagle, with his paw pads hitting the ground very hard. The moment he felt the impact,

Elite leaned his head down and let his whole body roll forward, maintaining a little momentum and reducing the spring shock through his bones. With that, Elite self-righted and sprinted for the thinner gaps between trees where the bear would be unable to follow without breaking them down first.

Wulfur navigated the long way back to Elite, using the trees as a shield before regrouping with him. The bear was flustered as both the targets had disappeared. He could hear and smell them, but continued to patrol the clearing, expecting them not to have gone far.

"Dumb bear," Wulfur said. This grabbed the beasts' attention once more and Wulfur made a dash for the swamp. Elite followed closely.

"Where's Naito?" Elite asked Wulfur. He didn't answer. "Father? Where is he?"

Wulfur huffed at his son as they both moved around the swamp. The old male barged Elite toward the right to avoid contact with the water.

"Don't worry about him," Wulfur answered, his tone holding softer than normal. Elite instantly stopped, smelling the air as he did so.

"What... what do you mean by that?" Elite asked.

His nose picked up Naito's last scent. It made him turn his head toward the swamp. There, before his eyes, was Naito's collapsed body with only the head submerged in the water. Elite was across the swamp from the lifeless corpse of his partner. He didn't scream, or shout for Naito. Instead, Elite silently gawped at his body. This was a wolf he liked, he trusted, he resonated with, now dead. Wulfur intervened with his commanding tone.

"Let's go, now!" he said.

"No..." Elite whispered to himself. Wulfur watched about a wolf's length from behind. Elite stepped forward, feeling an ache in his belly. Something was hurting him, and it made him begin running toward the swamp edge.

"Elite, stop! It's too late!" Wulfur shouted.

The golden wolf pinned his ears back, trying to muffle out his father's words. But then something did stop him. His claws scratched through the dirt and into the shallow part of the swamp when he saw a familiar ball of fur. It was the bear. It had gone around the open crest to get here and had dashed toward the bank where Naito laid. In panic, Elite scrambled his legs to run the opposite direction, back to Wulfur. His bag swayed and tugged at his neck with his rough manoeuvre.

"Go, go, go! The bear will be long distracted," Wulfur instructed, leading the way out of the fog. Elite followed, sorrow in his eyes, yet he didn't know that's what he was experiencing. Why did it hurt? How could having no physical pain allow for the sense of loss to hurt just as badly? He sighed in confusion, blindly following his father away from danger. They had left the swamp all alone to the bear, who had sat down and begun dismantling the limbs of the fallen Naito to satisfy its' hunger.

About an hour later, further through the woods, the trees had become lighter and thinner in profile. Although the sky was still dark, there were morning birds already singing their tunes. Wulfur led the way across, taking in the serenity and calm now that things seemed to be the way they were before. Elite trudged behind, keeping his nose aimed at the ground. He had his mouth slightly open, letting out occasional drips of saliva. His ears were held low, and his breathing was eerily gentle. Wulfur peered behind him to check if his son was still following closely enough to hear him. He noticed his stiff walk cycle and flattened his brows as he spoke.

"Don't think too much about him. Think about how much of our food we'd be made to share. He's a waste of resources. We don't need him. You... don't need him."

Wulfur slowed to make himself better heard by Elite. There was no acknowledgement of his teachings. "Did you hear what I said, Elite? He was going to be nothing but trouble."

They kept walking single file through the forest, finally finding the river that would lead them to the waterfall. Then Elite raised his head, glaring at Wulfur under his intimidating lowered brows. Elite's inner fury put a huge mask over his first experience of grief. His mind didn't understand how to react to such a feeling, so he resorted to his argumentative ways. But unlike before, he was more determined to get under his fathers' skin.

"You killed him, didn't you?" he spoke quietly but with a fiery tone. He snarled at Wulfur, exposing his canines.

"Does it matter?" Wulfur asked, stretching his neck back in annoyance. "Dusty boy had been assigned to kill you. It's good that he's gone."

Elite sped up to overtake his father before scooting around and standing in his way. Wulfur stopped and looked down at his son, who had posed himself rather cowardly despite the fumes coming from his head.

"GOOD?!" Elite shouted, the echo of his voice springing through the woods and silencing a few birds. "Whilst that is clearer to me now, yes, he decided *not* to. He changed his mind."

Elite furiously huffed in his father's face. "And it's Naito! Not dusty boy. Turns out that *was* his name before leaving his family, not by choice. Why don't you just tell me the truth? Stop lying! Did you kill him or didn't you?"

Elite's arrogance cracked a little, realising the notoriety of the wolf he was opposing. A killer at least. For a moment, Elite imagined his father's ability to vanquish *him* from the land of the living. Wulfur could do that at any time, and Elite wouldn't see it coming.

Wulfur simply scoffed at his pathetic son. He didn't see why this needed explaining. But perhaps Elite needed some kind of reminder that Naito was a burden to their plan.

"Yes, Elite. I did," Wulfur declared, his tone blunt but brutal. "Of course he didn't drown himself. I helped him out. Less of a problem for us. You see, Elite, he likes the Wise Wolf. There's every chance he would try to stop us because he's sympathetic, as he was towards you. You fell in love, and it made you weak!"

Elite flinched at the idea of death by drowning. Naito's fear must have been paramount. He struggled to picture Wulfur holding Naito under the water. It was horrifying, it was immoral. He grimaced at his father, every word out of his mouth felt like poison in Elite's ears.

"Now he's gone..." Wulfur continued with confidence. "...we can focus on our mission. The Wise Wolf really does have a major aspect influence. If we kill him, and their so-called messenger finds out, I will be the most feared wolf in the land. Even other animals will run for the hills when they hear me howling!" Wulfur advanced by navigating around Elite, who had loosened his legs whilst still growling under his breath.

Wulfur wanted to settle the score with Elite and regain his trust. But now was not the time. He knew that The Wise Wolf might escape if he knows they are coming, and survivors from the pack could be tracking them down right now. He was keen to know who this 'messenger' was that Oslo spoke of back at the den. A wolf who could tell other aspects the news and whereabouts of problems was more influential than the average scout.

"Listen..." Wulfur said to Elite, his back turned and heading off on a familiar path where he could narrowly see the waterfall a few miles North. "...once the Wise Wolf is dead, I'll make it up to you. We'll get you a proper mate. There's always a female wanderer out in the woods somewhere."

As the feeling of depression gripped him in the gut, Elite let his front paws slide against the dirt. He held the bow position stiff for a while as he reflected over his fathers' motives.

He knew a lot was possible being a loner. Very few rules stood in his father's way. But a talon rule stayed hard and true to Elite: No wolf could ever replace Naito. That wolf had given him some new experiences, including a faster heart rate in the presence of something comforting, followed by the pain in his heart when they were no longer with him. Getting up, Elite stalked after his father at a slower pace, trembling at the lips, knowing that his guide to the light had been extinguished forever.

Chapter 12

It turned dawn. A light array of pink clouds filled the sky. The silhouettes of trees in the dark began to show their true green of spring. On the opposite end of the field, about a mile South-East of the swamp, emerged Quade. He was walking with some form and was acquainted by another wolf. Her fur coat made her look like a silverware ornament that had gathered a large amount of dust. A few fur strands, white and soulless, found themselves detached and discarded from the females' pelt as she trotted alongside Quade. Her face had some tidy curly locks of fur, giving her a strikingly elegant look. She navigated the open terrain less confidently, her front legs often shaking slightly when she applied her lean weight on them.

Quade looked at her with a determined gaze.

"...and I told the alpha not to let them in! But he did it anyway."

The older female turned her head slowly, not blinking nor flicking her ears at the statement.

"Alpha Oslo has followed the Wise Wolf's guidance to his word. I said what I needed to say, Quade. I even gifted him a warning, but... you understand I have a lot going on between myself and the Wise Wolf, hm?"

Quade lowered his head, the truth hitting him like it had before, but never fully realised the weight of her situation.

"Yes, Imelda," he replied.

She gave Quade a slow blink before returning to look at her path ahead. Imelda could see a messy grey smoke hovering high above where the pack of unquiet dreams was based. It was eerie enough to fade the green from her eyes.

She continued to speak softly, not alerting Quade to the sight ahead.

"If we had come sooner, there would be something we could have done to stop them. But... I think we're too late." At the end of her sentence, she bopped her head up, signalling Quade to look across the field. He gawped.

"Raven raptures!" he exclaimed. "No... Jeeva! Alpha Oslo! Zavi!" Quade called out pack members as he began to sprint ahead of Imelda. He zoomed across the open field to reach the den entrance, its' bushes stripped of green and barely any branches left standing. Imelda fell behind, choosing to take her time.

Quade cracked burnt twigs beneath his paws as he moved hastily through the broken entrance. The clearing he remembered being so green, was now a thick layer of ash, the browner paths being all that remained of the den architecture. That, and Naito's hollow tree. The big, overgrown forest monster had survived the fires. The nursery den and the hunters' nests, however, were completely purged. The alpha's rock was dormant, and the prey pile was nothing more than an eerie pile of bones.

"Is any wolf here?" he cried out. For a moment, there was silence. Quade lowered his head, assuming the worst. Then, of all wolves, Alpha Oslo emerged from the entrance of Naito's den, limping his way up the short hill to confront Quade.

"Alpha!" he shouted in a mix of relief and shock. "What happened?!"

Alpha Oslo grunted in pain, his spine and legs feeling the damage dealt to him by Wulfur. Quade could see some of Liara's paw-work, the use of wrapping vines around limbs to stop bleeding.

Before Oslo could speak, Liara, Zavi and Jeeva came up from the den too. Jeeva was limping on her hind leg, which showed severe burns and fur loss. Quade brought his soft side to the forefront, seeing his trainee in such a state.

Zavi held his head low, his eyes fixated at the ground, ears pointed outward and a slight undertone growl coming from his jaw. Liara's expression was cold, whilst she had loose vines around her front paws.

Oslo slowly nodded at his allies behind before he turned to face Quade, the tone in his voice made sharp by the traumatic events burning through his head.

"Quade, the Goldfire. They intoxicated us with... a plant of some sort. I should have listened to you."

He let his head drop to below Quade's chest, a deep, regretful sigh escaping his breath.

"Where are the others?" Quade questioned, a lump beginning to form in his throat.

The Alpha slowly blinked at him before inhaling through his nose, his lip trembling lightly.

"There's only Arvux who's alive under the tree. All the others, they... perished."

Quade shook his head in disbelief. There was no way that could be true.

"You mean Sapphina's dead?... and Freya? Your mate?"

He let out a wineful gasp as the list in his head checked out for another few important individuals.

"Leyla and the pups too?" he whispered, not wanting to sound too invested in the death toll.

Oslo slowly nodded after each name. Zavi stomped his way forward alongside his alpha.

"My brother is gone too!" he growled with an enraged tone, his heart beating fast. "The Goldfire will pay for what they have done!"

Quade felt Zavi's tension burn right through him. He felt the same close connection with Jeeva, even though they weren't related. He saw Liara twitch her nose, trying to hold back from sobbing.

"I went to get, uh..." the mentor stopped, hearing the light tread of footsteps behind him. Imelda had arrived. She stood next to Quade with her shallow frown being targeted at Oslo.

"Where did you put the dead? And Naito? Where is he?" Quade asked, remembering that the young scout had been assigned to deal with the golden wolf.

Oslo sat down and held his head up to the pink sky. Imelda observed, her silent snarl intensifying at his ignorance.

"I don't know," the Alpha replied, gazing at the clouds. "We tried to look for him. The Goldfire went into his den after they set the grounds on fire. But when we got down there to shelter from the flames... they had disappeared. Naito too." Oslo held a steady tone whilst avoiding eye contact with any wolf in the group. "The bodies... they... we, uhm... they're under the tree. The ground is too hard to dig, so we let them float away in the lake."

Quade stared at Oslo, surprised by the responses. Liara let out a quiet but harsh snivel, followed by a whine.

"They were so young," she withered, the cold morning air making her shiver. Her comment triggered a moment of silence in the clearing. All the wolves' ears went erect, as if they were trying to hear voices in the wind. Maybe some answers from the Greater

Ones. But there was nothing. The group collectively lowered their heads in mourning, a couple peering over to the pile of burnt wood where the den mother, Leyla, used to watch over the pups.

"I think Naito teamed up with them," Zavi snapped at Oslo. His tail raised as he stood up abruptly. "I want some fresh blood. We should hunt them down."

"No, no, hold on..." Liara interrupted, leaning her head forward past Zavi. "We're barely a pack anymore. If we lose more wolves, we'll have to go our own ways." She sounded very worried in her light tone, her paws itching at the loose bandages. "I don't want to look for another home. Alpha, you said this was our purpose in the advancement against the humans."

Oslo's ear flicked at Liara's voice, her words hurting his reputation. He knew the Wise Wolf had told him to do all these things. The Wise Wolf had promised them a lot. He needed to come clean about the situation.

"Listen, Liara. All of you," Oslo said, returning to Earth with his nose and swaying his stare at each wolf in sight, but finding his ears to drop when the wolf of focus was Imelda, who looked the least pleased. "The Wise Wolf made me believe his words. He is, as every wolf knows, the wolf of guidance. Why his guidance failed me, I don't know. The Greater Ones probably have the answers."

"Does this mean the Wise Wolf is a liar?" Quade asked, his head tilting to the left.

"No, it doesn't," Imelda interrupted, making Quade dart his head toward her, the other wolves focusing on the silver female in unison. "The Wise Wolf's wisdom can be dangerous. The truth isn't always a blessing. And part of his role is to shield us from knowledge that could kill us!" She took a slight step forward and sat directly in front of Oslo, their noses separated by a ferret's length. Her tone lightened whilst her eyes remained ominously serious. "I think our Alpha could have avoided this."

She waited for Oslo to look at her directly in the eyes before speaking again. Oslo did exactly that. "I warned you, Oslo. You didn't bring your hunters in to help because the Wise Wolf told you to deal with Wulfur by yourself. He still has a grudge on you, don't you remember?"

Oslo stared with a face of regret, before his eyes began to look at the ground, trying to escape what Imelda was telling him. She continued. "That night at the Howling Dawn. He never forgot. But you're only alive because you never knew his name."

The whole group sat silently as Imelda finished giving Oslo a recap of past events. Zavi's claws were digging into the ground, and Liara was aiming her snout at the Alpha, waiting for orders. Just then, a familiar laugh came from under the tree. They all looked over to see Arvux bouncing happily out of Naito's bruised den.

"WOW! What an evening!" He shouted. "There was so much light, and hot! OW! It still burns!" The jester wolf bounced around with his tail tip all black and crispy.

Oslo regained some of his ego and leaned his head back.

"Hey, I told you to wait under the tree," Oslo reminded to Arvux.

Quade frowned at the familiar jester wolf, who clearly had no idea of the situation and its' toll. Being blissfully unaware like Arvux was. That was a curse by itself. But then his eyes widened. He flicked an ear away from Imelda. A dark smile appeared on his face before he hid it under a tone of desperation. He raised a paw and pointed it at Arvux who was still prancing around like a horse out of control.

"It's Arvy's fault!" Quade called out. "He told the Goldfire where to find our pack. He told them everything!"

The group exchanged looks of doubt before taking a peep at Arvux and his funny behaviour. Arvux stopped for a moment after hearing his name and he firmly sat down with his tongue out. "Ooh, what? Me? Yeah, I, wait... I told who what now?"

Jeeva, with all her remaining strength, navigated past Zavi to stand beside Arvux.

"It's not his fault, he doesn't know any better. We could have killed them anyway if the Alpha..." Jeeva stopped, realising she was about to challenge Oslo, the wolf who raised her to be a hunter, and in front of Quade who had mentored her for so long. She looked around for a resolve, then felt her heart sink. "Arvux didn't do anything he wasn't allowed to do- OW!" she whimpered, putting a paw around her brother's shoulders and the other on her sore leg. Arvux glanced over with his usual playful grin.

Oslo weighed his decision in his head. Yes, Arvux was nuts, but did that mean he could be held accountable for the whole problem? It was, after all, possible for the pack to have gotten away without being discovered.

"We should cast him out," Quade said loudly and proudly, his neck gaining stiffness alongside his raised eyebrows and low smirk.

"Quade!" Jeeva cried, attempting to scold him for suggesting such a solution. But that was when Oslo looked at Jeeva and raised a paw, displaying his torn pads at her.

"Enough, Jeeva," Oslo ordered. "You know that this was going to happen to him anyway. And yes, Zavi..." he looked over to the sole remaining brute hunter. "...you shall go after the Goldfire. Take Imelda and Quade with you. Me and Jeeva will stay here. We still need to heal."

"But Alpha..." Quade opposed, giving Oslo a stern look. "That would be a paw and talon on each side. We might not win. Especially if Naito rebels against us."

Alpha Oslo got up and began to trot toward the entrance, speaking with a commanding tone.

"I know. But it's the only hope we have left of restoring this pack. Either kill them and get back the food they stole. Or die trying." He slowed to turn his head, seeing Imelda had also risen to follow him, along with an eager Zavi and a bouncing Arvux. "The ancestors have put us under a test of survival. If we prevail, we will surely be rewarded."

Behind the group, Liara sat still whilst Jeeva leaned against her, whining under her brisket.

"But he's my brother," Jeeva whispered with a tremble in her lips.

"I know, dearest. And I am so sorry," Liara replied, opening her legs further to comfort the mourning red wolf.

Imelda increased her pace and navigated around the Alpha. Her proximity was tighter than what was comfortable for both parties. A witch-like tone grumbled out of her mouth.

"Regret not making me the healer?" Imelda said to Oslo. "If I was never a messenger, you wouldn't be in this mess."

She gave Oslo a quick, distasteful glance before taking the lead out of the den and back into the open field. Oslo shook away Imelda's words like snow on his ears. He regained a sense of authority when he saw to Zavi, Arvux and Quade on their way out.

"Go around the trees, find that long path and try to pick up their scent," Oslo said delicately. "Bring back their tails as a souvenir for me, Zavi. Quade, I'll leave you in charge of casting out Arvux. Place him somewhere... out of harm's way."

Arvux heard his name again and was super excited to follow Quade out the entrance.

"Are we going on another scout mission? Are we? Are we?! Ooh, that sounds just like my name! Are we, Arvy? Haha!"

"I will, Alpha," Quade said almost in sync with Zavi, his faith feeling restored in his duties with Oslo. "Yes, Arvux. We're heading North to a special training spot."

"YIPPEE!" Arvux squeaked, bouncing in joy behind Quade's tail. "I can't wait to be such a skilled scouter. Is that what I'm called? Ooh, we are going now. Alright!"

Imelda led the group without another word to Oslo, her tail dominantly poised outward and leaving a silver wave of fur for the others to follow. Zavi walked up front with Imelda, his expression nothing short of vengeful.

"When we find them, I'm going to make them sorry. Make them beg for their miserable lives before slicing their throats," Zavi vowed to himself, looking into Imelda's eyes for approval of his intentions. The older female kept her gaze ahead, but taking in the tough situation Zavi must be going through. Losing a sibling wasn't any new story to her.

Oslo sat down at the entrance, seeing the group venture out, on a hunt for the Goldfire. The damage was done, and Oslo could only beg for forgiveness from the ancestors. He looked up at the fluffy clouds, seeing little hope reflect through his eyes.

"Greater Ones, if you're listening, what did my pack do to deserve this? Why did you let my mates die in agony? Freya and Leyla. And pups of all things. My hunter Fenn and scout Sapphina have also perished. Have I been told a lie? Is the pack hierarchy also fake?"

After a few seconds of silence in the wind, Oslo sighed and looked down to see the group had already disappeared. Without the full moon, or a spirit gate to connect to, he knew he wouldn't be receiving answers anytime soon. All he could do was ask more questions.

But he had a task to do for himself. Heal up, get strong and attempt to salvage this pack he had built and nurtured for years. He grumbled under his breath before facing his charred pack grounds. Liara sat there in the lifeless open with Jeeva pressed against her shoulder. A foul aura of smoke filled the air from the burned forage as Oslo joined them for comfort and grieving.

Following on into the dark forest, Imelda had her nose on the ground, familiar as she was to most of the local territories. The daylight made it easier to see through the swampy mist. Zavi had dropped back whilst Quade had neared up to Imelda. Arvux joyfully sprung up and down from behind them.

"So, what did you mean by that? What you said to the Alpha," asked Quade, ears poised to absorb any information Imelda hadn't told him before.

"Oh, about his connection to the Wise Wolf? Nothing, really," Imelda said. "Oslo might have just gotten in his way as a pup."

"And what about you?" Quade asked. "The Wise Wolf was your mate, right? You know his name. What is it?" His eyes widened, glaring at Imelda with unquiet intrigue. She stopped walking forward to confront the question posed by Quade.

"Look, Quade," Imelda began, her tone as mysterious as the wind. "I said it before, and I'll say it again: the truth isn't always a blessing. The Greater Ones are more powerful than we're made to realise. The reason Oslo isn't already dead, the reason he is your Alpha today, is because he never learned the Wise Wolf's name."

"But you know his name," Quade counter argued. "How come *you* aren't dead?"

Imelda's eyes softened, almost sorrowful toward Quade. For a moment, Imelda was utterly still, the weight of what she could not say had anchored her in silence. Her lips parted, but no words came.

A loud disruption from behind broke the suspense. The rapid rustling of leaves and uncontrollable giggling made the pair look over to Arvux. Imelda simply closed her mouth and resumed walking, whilst Quade faced the crazy wolf with a disapproving grunt.

"Are we there yet?" Arvux yelled. "Ha, just kidding!"

Quade shook himself free from Imelda's silence and trotted awkwardly, letting go of the unanswered question. He needed to get back on track with the task at hand: Lose Arvux and then kill the Goldfire… and maybe Naito too.

"Almost," Quade answered to Arvux.

Zavi looked around, his nose also taking in details about this forest. He could smell a bear, swampy water, and blood. Fresh blood. Then Zavi found himself nearing an odd crest amongst the trees but noticed the group taking a detour to the West. He grunted before turning away from the crest to chase after them, preventing him from advancing to the swamp where Naito's bones laid.

They soon arrived at a sloped descent; a few miles shy of the highlands. It resembled a supersized ditch in the earth that looked useable as a trap.

"We are here," Quade said, gently padding against the edge. "Slide down there, close your eyes and count to a feathanest. When you are done, come and find us. That's the assignment."

"Ooh, okay!" he responded with glee, sprinting toward the drop and then proceeding to slide down on his paws. He picked up so much speed that he lost balance and collapsed in a fluffy bread pile at the bottom.

"I'm okay!" he said, raising his head from the dirt. "I'm going to start counting, so you better run!"

"And no peeking! We'll be somewhere nearby," Quade called down at the young jester wolf.

"Of course not, Quade," Arvux assured, closing his eyes. "Here I go! A talon, a paw, a talon and paw, half a nest... uhh... hm, let me think what comes next..."

Above him, Quade walked away from the edge with a dark smile on his face.

"Let's go," he whispered at the others. Zavi had little reaction to the decision. But Imelda went up to the edge to watch Arvux for a moment.

"He isn't going to survive on his own," she quietly told herself.

"Come on, let's move before he finds us," Quade called out from the thick of the swampy forest behind her. Imelda regretfully huffed and turned away from the crazy wolf, catching up to the others, her shiny pelt fading into the forest depths like a ghost.

Arvux continued counting whilst he squinted his eyes tightly.

"Oh, that's right, a pawpa-talon. Then it's a feathapaw. That's my favourite count. Um... alright! I think I've counted long enough. I'm coming, ready or not!"

He opened his eyes and began to dart around the huge bowl of greenery, looking for Quade, or the others, if they were playing the game as well.

"Haha, you can't hide forever, I'm so good at this game!"

He continued searching, unaware of his inability to escape the ditch, looking for wolves that weren't hiding there at all. He would keep searching... and searching... until boredom would get the better of him. He sat down and began to scratch his ear.

"Uh, Quade, I give up... um... what game were we playing again? Heh, fellow wolves? Where did you go?"

It had only been a few minutes and Quade was long gone into the forest, following the scent of the Goldfire. His fun was over. Getting rid of Arvux felt good. But they now had to eliminate the threats that were set to oppose them.

Imelda led the way with her nose, now aiming East in line with the river. She stopped and looked ahead, eyes widening with concern. Her glare was focused solely on the distant horizon where the river met with the sky.

"What is it?" Zavi asked, keeping pumped up and energised, ready to pounce on his enemies.

Imelda turned to respond to the pair of males.

"They're going after the Wise Wolf. We must hurry."

The trio took off in a canter-sprint along the river, bound for the waterfall that Imelda was sure the Goldfire were headed.

Chapter 13

The sight of the sun sent a wave of yellow mist over the waterfall and the trees. It blurred the horizon with a warm yet unsettling aura. At the crest, the Wise Wolf stared down toward the South side of the river that flowed away from him. He saw less trees than yesterday. For him, they seemed to have vanished overnight. A light gust blew underneath him, his tail catching it like a net to a butterfly.

His ears turned to the sides, hearing a sharp pitter-patter of paws crawling up the riverbank behind him. He slowly turned to face the threat, his rigid body eclipsing the sun. It was the Goldfire. Wulfur had returned with his son. The Wise Wolf exhaled suppressively, mostly focusing on Wulfur, leading the charge as he had done before.

"You have a lot of nerve coming back," the Wise Wolf muttered eerily. "What is it that you seek?"

The timber male's fangs exposed from under his enraged glare.

"Drop the act, faker," Wulfur started, his approach slowing and paw placement more precise. "You made Oslo believe in some crazy pecking order. Your lies brought their downfall and now I'm going to end you."

He stopped, taking a second to drop the bag of prey and push it aside with his paw. Elite cowered behind, his hocks jittering and tail tucked under. The Wise Wolf scoffed at Wulfur.

"Ha, your threats don't make up for your incompetence," explained the Wise Wolf. He knew keeping the peace would be hard, but he had a second plan if Wulfur didn't comply. "You see how easy it is to manipulate wolves who group together not knowing who to trust? Humans and the ancestors? I've seen it all."

The Wise Wolf turned a little bit more, allowing the sunlight to peer over his back, making Wulfur squint his eyes. He took a step closer, exposing even more teeth.

"I know the truth of the Greater Ones," the Wise Wolf continued. "That doesn't mean I always speak it. Oslo was such a gullible pup. If wolves are lost enough, they'll believe me, and follow my guidance wherever it leads. Even through the dark."

Wulfur gripped his claws into the dirt and snarled, his snout pulled back like flesh from bone.

"Cut it out with your false wisdom!" Wulfur snapped. "You're done!"

"What are you going to do?" the Wise Wolf asked, his focus now shifting to the young golden male behind Wulfur. "Get your nameless son to fight this time? He still doesn't seem to trust you. This is your last warning. Walk away now, or you will have chosen death."

Wulfur paused his verbal taunting, noticing the confidence the Wise Wolf evoked. He wouldn't allow him to walk away alive, which only made him feel more envious of his reputation. The way he paused between breaths. The way he eyed behind him at his son. It made his jaw ache from growling so hard.

Without answering, Wulfur barked and then charged at the Wise Wolf, who was ready for it this time. He barked back and parried Wulfur's attack. The timber male's teeth grinded through the black fur on the Wise Wolf's brisket. When Wulfur pulled away, the pair circled slowly as Elite watched from the safety of a few grass bristles near the rocky riverbank.

"Come on, Elite," Wulfur called out without turning his head. "Let's kill him!"

But the golden wolf remained hunched in the green. Elite still had his bag over his shoulder with part of the human rifle sticking out. As the fighting pair rotated, the Wise Wolf had a quick glimpse at Elite to see if he would try anything.

"See? You're a terrible father," the Wise Wolf mused, returning to Wulfur. "I sense his potential, and you have done nothing but drain that out of him. And you finally named him. Congratulations on that." He couldn't help but smirk at Wulfur, knowing the last encounter ended embarrassingly.

Wulfur, now with his back turned from the drop, made an impulse lunge to get at the Wise Wolf for his words. "SHUT IT!" Wulfur bellowed mid-charge.

The Wise Wolf ducked his head and collected Wulfur's chin between his ears. With all his strength, the Wise Wolf bounced upward, forcing Wulfur's body to jump with him toward the sky. Their paws got off the ground as the Wise Wolf's forehead was pressed against Wulfur's throat. The Wise Wolf's legs accurately padded against his enemy whilst theirs flailed crazily. Wulfur hit the rock hard with his rigid spine, his head close to the edge. The sound of gushing water filled his left ear.

Elite twitched at every move the fighting wolves made. The aggression spiked through his eyes, fuelling self-preservation in his mind. If he didn't fight, he would be unharmed at the end.

Then he thought of his place if Wulfur came out on top. Elite would surely be shunned for life for not aiding him. Elite began to shake his legs at the thought of Wulfur killing him for disloyalty.

The only thing he could do here was prove he had that loyalty. He could die trying to help, but for whatever the ancestors turned out to be, he would have made a valiant effort to deserve the good side of the afterlife. The fight continued to ensue as Elite crouched apprehensively in the background.

Wulfur winced as he tried to get back to his feet, but then felt the sting of claws press against his belly, pinning him down. He looked up to see the fury of the Wise Wolf burning down on him.

"Hardly a challenge," the Wise Wolf mocked at Wulfur. "I'm sure the local aspects will enjoy hearing of your bravery."

Wulfur inhaled, gargling saliva that he didn't have the energy to swallow. His bare fangs retracted momentarily to think of those aspects. Their encounters with him and Elite. He remembered that the Wise Wolf knew of their actions.

"Who is your messenger?!" Wulfur demanded, his guttered voice going to a new low. "Giving another wolf your dirty work. You're not just a liar, you're also raviking lazy!"

The Wise Wolf blinked at the question as a pinch of unease reshaped his brows. Breathing in to get energy back, he answered to Wulfur's curiosity with his wise old tone.

"She is my mate. I've known her since I was young. A lot of wolves find themselves dead getting comfortable around me. But not her, though. You don't need the details. That's just how it is."

His mate. That was very strange. Especially if she didn't know the Wise Wolf's name. The desire to meet her and learn the truth amplified his confidence. Wulfur may have been put in a precarious position, but he still had it in him to threaten the Wise Wolf.

"It would be a shame if she found you dead," Wulfur barked. "I'll have her follow my orders instead."

A dark smile painted itself over the Wise Wolf followed by a small huff.

"I'm sorry to say that it doesn't look like that will happen. I speak the truth, and this is your grave." He gave Wulfur a look that resembled that of an executioner. His fragile consciousness hidden under the mask of black fur, hungry for slaughter in the name of wolven democracy.

"Hey, Wise Wolf!"

The abrupt shout came from behind the pair. The Wise Wolf chose to keep Wulfur pinned as he turned his head. He caught a glimpse of gold hurtling toward him. Elite, now unladen by the duffel bag, charged into the Wise Wolf, virtually mounting him from behind. The golden wolf's smaller size allowed him to cling on to the Wise Wolf with his rear paws elevated off the ground.

Elite tasted the fur and the blood of his target. He knew he scored big with this bite, so he gnawed at the spine harder, wanting more. All the while, he kept his eyes closed, preventing any fear over the large drop.

The Wise Wolf felt Elite's teeth dig into his upper spine and he growled in response. He didn't feel much pain from the amateur bite. Just a desire to shake him off like a snowflake. The Wise Wolf bucked his rear legs, trying to discard the much smaller, lighter male. Elite's agile capable body remained locked. The old wolf felt blood being drawn from his back and he eventually pirouetted off Wulfur.

"Ah, big mistake, golden boy," the Wise Wolf said to Elite before whipping his rear toward the stricken timber male, who saw his chance to recover. Wulfur scrambled to his feet and tried to dive under the Wise Wolf, taking a bite at his left metatarsals whilst blinded by Elite's flappy tail.

The Wise Wolf let out a painful yelp and gyrated full circle near the drop, finally forcing Elite to lose his grip and fling off. Elite smacked sideways toward the crest, similarly to Wulfur, only this time his head leaned over the edge and fear filled his eyes. Along with the pain from his hard landing, Elite could see the massive cloud of water vapor that hid the waterfall's base from view.

Wulfur had regained his strength and watched the Wise Wolf backpedal nearer Elite.

"Get away from him!" he shouted at the Wise Wolf.

"Too late," the Wise Wolf replied, giving a firm, deliberate backwards kick at Elite's flank. Elite rolled off the edge and plummeted into the mist. Wulfur's eyes widened as he could only hear his son scream for a moment, followed by a muffled splash. Wulfur's silence was haunting. He then averted his eyes from the cliff to confront the Wise Wolf, again.

The black wolf that stood before him was also quiet. Perhaps he was waiting for Wulfur to show a sign of weakness, a sign of regret. The loss of his son wasn't going to change anything!

"You'll suffer for this!" Wulfur growled, his front legs ready to pounce back at the killer of his own flesh and blood.

But the Wise Wolf stood calm and collected, looking indirectly at Wulfur.

"Like I said, you're too late. No matter what you do, you're dead."

Wulfur took notice of the Wise Wolf's stare and realised it wasn't on him. Something behind him. The temptation to look was immense, but it couldn't be true. He wouldn't fall for it. The Wise Wolf had to be tricking him.

They both remained static, Wulfur waiting for the Wise Wolf to be busted for his lie yet again. But the Wise Wolf himself curved an evil grin as the reflection of his eye caught a white sparkle in the forest behind them. Wulfur saw this and felt his heart drop, holding his breath as the flare moved.

At the base, the fog combined with the chute of water made for a pool of chaos. A few yards in front of the water's landing point came some bubbles. Then, suddenly, a golden jaw burst to the surface, wide open for the immediate contact with air. It was Elite. He gasped desperately as he felt the chill from being soaked as well as walking on nothing underneath him. Elite's legs scrambled, eventually finding some rhythm in the gushing water and slowly made his way to the North side of the riverbank. Blinded and confused, he coughed and spat, ejecting droplets back into the river.

Elite dragged himself onto dry land among the short grass and collapsed sideways like a corpse. His chest pounded in and out as he felt the sense of fear become dormant. He had survived the fall. He knew that he was lucky the waterfall wasn't larger or had sharp rocks to boast at the bottom. That would have killed him for sure. His rapid breathing inhaled the scent of the dry dirt beneath him, a reminder that he was safe, and not drowning.

Suddenly, a loud bang echoed through the air. Elite's ears erected instantly, and his eyes widened in a nanosecond. Elite recognised that sound from the site where he tricked his father about killing the deer. That was the sound of death. A black magic weapon. *'The humans are here?'* he thought. Flocks of birds evacuated from their trees and the rest of the forest went silent.

He raised his head to see if he could identify anything from the crest above. The deep, strained voice of his father called out for the Wise Wolf.

"Rarrrgh, I'm not dying like this. Come back here! What else do you know?!"

Elite then heard the rush of paws come down the hillside toward him, where the crest descended into the forest. Looking ahead, Elite saw the figure of the Wise Wolf dash down the forest edge, following the river. Elite's attention remained on the Wise Wolf's escape until he heard his father's voice again, the tone turning more desperate.

"No! Stay away from me!"

The golden male struggled up to his feet and shook off the water in his pelt. He then limped his way up the hill to regroup with his father, whatever was happening to him.

As he climbed to the top, a strange tall figure had made itself present in front of Wulfur. Was this... a human? He was within a dozen metres before the human noticed. Elite could now see the full scale of the outcome. Wulfur was collapsed, his rear leg bleeding violently from a huge hole and his body withering in pain. The human held a contraption, same as in Elite's bag.

"Elite!" Wulfur cried in relief. "You're alive. Quick, attack the human!"

The golden male was immobile, staring at the eyes of the sub-gods. A fighter from the great war with the Greater Ones, as it was told. He watched the hunter panic with his unique limbs, scrambling for an item on his self. He appeared to pull out a bullet from his own carry bags, quite alike the object from Naito's collection, and fiddled to put it inside the rifle.

Elite stood very still, up until the point the hunter had finished reloading and pointed the barrel directly at him. The golden male then slowly lowered to a crouch, a light grumble escaping his mouth. The contraption was pointing at him. Just like Wulfur had described before, this meant that he was dead. He braced himself for the power of humanity to meet his senses.

But, before the hunter could pull the trigger, he heard a yelp from behind. A light voice with a touch of innocence, but the language inaudible to Elite. A young human child emerged from the forest walls and approached the hunter. Elite returned to standing upright as he recognised the young human. It was the child who unlocked the food cabinet back at the camp for him. The pair of humans appeared to be discussing something.

Elite couldn't understand. He had only distorted 'Ooh's and 'Aah's to take in, but it wouldn't ever translate into anything useful. All he could do was watch and think about his father. Could *any* wolf survive that injury? The presence of humans made both their fates feel unavoidable.

After a few glances and sudatory exchanges, the hunter lowered his weapon and nodded his head at Elite. All the while, Wulfur continued to whine and grunt as the ground beneath him continued to fill in red.

"Elite, help me! I'm not dying here!"

Elite then started to walk slowly around the humans, careful not to appear hostile. The young child watched in fascination as Elite navigated to their right. Elite focused on the bag with the other rifle inside and picked it up with his teeth. He returned to the group, stood perfectly between Wulfur and the humans. Elite placed the bag down and pulled the zipper to reveal the contents. He dug his nose in and bit into the dreamcatcher Naito had designed.

"Here," Elite said through gritted teeth. "My friend wanted you to have this." He didn't know if the humans understood him. Probably not. But he could only approach like this if the conversation was friendly enough. The young boy took a step forward and held his hands out willingly. Elite froze, not expecting such a positive response. Every move he was cautious, yet very ignorant of his injured father. Elite let go of the trinket, so it fell into the child's open hands. He was a little bit scared to touch those unique limbs. They looked complex and clever.

Wulfur gawped whilst trying to wriggle some life into his paralysed leg. Elite appeared to be befriending the humans. This was not normal. It wasn't allowed. He *wouldn't* allow it! Wulfur's whines of pain turned into frustrated growls, trying to reach for the tail of his son.

Elite heard his fathers' growling and turned only his head, bringing him into the corner of his eye. The golden male huffed, tactfully kicking dirt and scent at Wulfur with his rear paws. A sense of self-comfort filled the golden male, knowing he could do that without consequence.

Then the hunter also stepped forward, leaning his back over to look inside the bag. His long arm reached down to grab the rifle. Elite noticed him taking a keen eye to its' details. He was almost the same as when Naito observed it. Very keen, yet ominously knowledgeable with such tools.

The hunter then raised the weapon with an alien grip and placed it behind him. Elite turned to face the humans again. His heart rate increased at the sight of the hunter momentarily holding, not a talon's worth, but a paw's worth of black magic contraptions. Elite watched the hunter's spare hand then aim toward him. The human hand hovered over Elite's nose. '*What was the hunter doing? Was there something on his hand? Did he want me to smell it?'*

And then Elite lowered his head, too afraid to touch. He let the human do what they wanted. Sensing the hunter's approach, Elite tried looking at the young child to distract himself. *'Maybe this was his father,'* Elite thought. He had never been sure that the sub-gods had bloodline relations, but here, it appeared to be true.

Elite then felt a rush of senses tingle him as the hunters' hand grazed at his scalp and ruffled behind his ears. The golden male felt it tickle to begin with, each point on the end of the hunters' hand carving through his fur like a fish through water. Then it felt surprisingly pleasant. Elite closed his eyes and leaned his head up, feeling the pressure increase against his skull. It was especially blissful when those pointy bits crawled behind his ears.

The child made another sound, like he was signalling his father. The hunter then stopped and saw the child pointing at Wulfur. The old timber male had stretched his neck far enough to see the group from where he was paralysed. The pair of humans made more gestures and sounds at each other.

"Elite, what are you doing?!" Wulfur yelled angrily.

Elite rotated away from the humans and spoke to Wulfur, his voice translating as a nasty snarl to the sub-gods.

"Father, I'm not helping you. We have failed." Elite began to snarl back at his father, his spine curving upward like a bent stick. "The Wise Wolf was right about you. You've been awful to me! All those lies! Blinding me from society. For moons! Making me your little backbone. Well, I'm done!"

The golden male then untensed his shoulders and approached Wulfur closer with his tail in the air.

"You remember when I said I hid in the forest after you beat me?" Elite gave a threatening smirk at his father, who observed with a gawp and winced eyes. "Well, I lied. Those bears weren't fighting us. They were fighting each other. I followed a crow to a distant den and rested there..."

Elite recalls the events in his head of the moment after he followed the crow away from the swampy forest. He was led into a monstrous collage of bushes. There, he was made welcome by many other crows, possibly related to the individual he had been following. They made markings in the ground with their talons, hinting at a story involving a pair of wolves and the diversity of woodland creatures.

The murder of crows tended to his wounds, giving him a sense of care for these creatures. In the middle of the night, he doesn't sleep. When the thought of his father raised, his face turned ugly. Elite is seen leaving the camp in the morning, marching to the pack with a new outlook toward the wild.

Returning to the crest, Elite gave his father a face of disapproval before turning to face the humans.

"You're getting everything you deserve, Wulfur. Now you're weak, I have a chance to do what *I* want."

The old timber male couldn't believe what he was hearing. Elite called him by his name instead of his father. He watched Elite face the humans and give them a low nod before leaving the bag of human goods where they were. The hunter returned the nod, readying the rifle he pointed at Elite earlier with. This time the target was Wulfur. The child stepped back and kept his focus on Elite rather than the kill.

"Elite, by the ancestors, there's no way you're letting this happen! The Greater Ones, they're coming after you! You won't survive on your own..." Wulfur strained his voice to the limit to make sure Elite heard good and proper. "...and that's why you will never escape!"

Those last words made Elite slow his pace as he headed for the bag of prey. He picked it up and slung it over his neck. Then, he made his final glance at his father who had guided him all his life, now at the mercy of the sub-gods. The young child waved at him before Elite disappeared behind the thick of the trees, Northside of the river.

Wulfur violently wriggled, using every muscle in his body to attempt an evasion of his fate. His growl turned from aggressive to desperate as the golden glow of his son faded into the forest.

Elite trotted with his food bag for a few seconds when, once again, a loud bang channelled its' way through the green, ringing in his ears. That was it. His father was dead.

Elite stopped for a moment to think. Wulfur was gone. His internal confidence had peaked moments ago. Why did it feel absent right now? The eeriness of having no wolf by his side, with no real goal to achieve, was slightly chilling. That last bang changed everything for Elite. He was free, but he needed to work out what he was free to do. He could try to join an aspect, but he felt like he wouldn't fit in. Elite thought of Naito, and how he had accomplished his mission by bringing the humans his dreamcatcher. And was it true that the Greater Ones would come after him for letting his father die?

This was all getting to his head, and he let out a sigh. Elite wanted to feel relief. The loss of being under another wolf's shadow didn't feel as satisfying as he'd imagined. With that, he set off with the bag of food, using the best of his memory and senses to find the hill toward the west, the very place he became interested in after his encounter with Arvux.

Remembering the pack, he began to move faster through the forage. He still had their food and would be easy to track. It was a shame to leave the Wise Wolf's beautiful gem cave behind, but Elite's survival depended on never returning there.

High above, a crow could be seen gliding in a similar direction, the wings working harmoniously with the wind. Slowly and steadily, it watched over the golden wolf in the woods.

Half an hour had passed since Elite's escape from the waterfall and the chasing group finally arrived on the scene. The stench of blood was rich, but absolutely no sign of wolven life. Imelda didn't let the scent fill her nostrils too much, while Zavi was keen to investigate. The blood was omnipotent with Wulfur's scent as he took a close whiff at the waterfall crest. But there wasn't any sign of Wulfur, Elite or their bags of goodies.

Meanwhile, Quade dashed down the hillside to check out the cave under the plunge. Imelda slowed to a tiptoe, her ears alert for any signs of movement. She slowly diverted from the path Quade took and kept following the river a little way down.

"There doesn't appear to be any wolf here," Quade called out. "Not even the Wise Wolf himself."

Imelda trotted up to a small assembly of rocks right on the edge of the riverbank, where the flow was gentler. She sat next to them and pushed her paw against the largest rock. Zavi soon came down to see Imelda, a look of satisfaction and envy in his eyes.

"I smell humans. Your suspicions were right," Zavi confirmed with Imelda. "That loud noise we heard. He must have died from it. The young wolf was here too, but no sign of Naito's scent."

Imelda looked up at Zavi with a straight face, the rock now pushed off its foundation. In its place was a squashed heather with all its pink bell-shaped petals intact. Imelda sighed, a little smile contemplating the release of worry. Quade dashed out of the cave to join them.

"What of the Wise Wolf? Where is he?" Quade asked, also looking down at the odd flower arrangement buried into the ground.

Imelda's mouth twitched at the corner, as though suppressing something. She then spoke with her lips flattened. "Dead."

Her word hung in the air for a bit. The tweeting of evening birds filled the silence along with a cool breeze, making Imelda's curly cheek fur flutter around.

"So... what about Naito? Or the gold wolf? Do we chase after them now?" Zavi asked with the smell of blood causing his primal energy to manifest.

Imelda stood up and took a breath of fresh air, then shook her ageing pelt, letting more stray fur fly away.

"We can't. Not if the humans are around. It's not safe. We return to Oslo and report who's dead and who's missing. I'm sorry to disappoint, Zavi."

Zavi rose to his feet and rolled his eyes, sticking close with Imelda. Quade took the lead up the hill with a concerned expression, bound for the place they called home, fallen to Wulfur's destruction. Imelda gave both male wolves a reassuring glance.

"Naito and the golden wolf. I'm sure the Greater Ones will guide them to their death, *if* they deserve it."

As the forest began to feel unfamiliar, Elite slowed to reflect. *'My father is dead, and now I'm alone. All by myself. I can do what I want...'* he breathed hastily as he felt a shiver between his shoulders. *'...and I can go where I want. He's not here to stop me.'* Elite looked behind him, too far gone to see the waterfall. It was over.

After slowly regaining his confidence to march on, Elite arrived at the peak of the hill. He saw the vast landscape that lie before him. An unexplored region of the world. This vast, open, interesting and dangerous world. He could see trees for miles and, in the distant horizon on his left, the mountains.

Elite gulped at another thought tracing back. Would Wulfur's last words haunt him? He did not have much knowledge on the Greater Ones, but their forces certainly felt...real. The next full moon, he would have to try howling at it.

The golden male heard a squawk and looked up to see the crow that had guided him all this way. For the first time on his own, he smiled and made his last glimpse at the territory he was departing from. Then he took a deep breath and began traversing in the direction *he* wanted to go. He brought with him the unique bag to carry food in, and, unknowingly, being followed by whispers in the wind.

Dusk had come and it shaded a hue of orange over the human settlement. Many vehicles were loaded with resources and lights were being switched off all around the camp. The hunter, the human who had encountered Elite, stared around the empty cabin before being called by another human. It was time to leave. He glimpsed at the family photo from inside the duffel bag before folding it up and sliding it into his pocket.

   He paused for a moment in the cabin, feeling an unnatural gust of wind shake the light bulb and the curtains. He felt the need to take another item out of his other pocket. It was a used bullet cartridge. He rubbed the tip against his chin whilst admiring a fur coat hanging from a wooden chair. A light brown coat with shades of timber and a dusty pattern of cocoa. He put the bullet away, picked up the coat, switched off the light and closed the door behind him. The natural light in the cabin turned a shade of violet as it was left in an eerie silence.

Printed in Great Britain
by Amazon